# *Hannah's Man*

*Rita Hestand*

# *Hannah's Man*

(Book Three of the Travers Brothers Series)

By Rita Hestand

**Smashwords Edition**

*Hannah's Man*



Digital ISBN # 9781700322258

Cover art by: Swoon Worthy Book Covers

## *Dedication:*

To all the young couples who wait faithfully for their wedding night to have sex, this book is dedicated to you. God Bless

*Rita Hestand*

# Table of Contents

## *Books in this Series*

Chief Cook & Bottle Washer
Courting Abby
Hannah's Man
Along Came Love
Avalanche of the Heart

# *Chapter One*

The cold north wind slashed across Rusty's face like a sharp slap, as he pulled his sheepskin jacket closer and marched to the ranch house as though the devil himself were chasing him. Rusty drew breath. He wondered why Deke had sent word to come to the house. Must be something important to have pulled him off post hole digging, Rusty pondered as he dusted his boots off before entering the house. His hands felt numb and he could barely turn the knob.

Warmth invaded him as he opened the door; the flickering firelight invited him in. Home sweet home, he smiled as he let the warmth seep slowly through him. He moved deliberately toward the welcoming fire and saw his brother standing resolutely at the big window, staring out. Noticing the tense stance, the vague greeting, and the silence in the room, Rusty knew there was something wrong. He took his hat off and smoothed his thick russet hair back, then replaced his hat.

"Deke, something wrong?" Rusty watched his brother closely as he shrugged out of his jacket and thrust his hands out toward the welcome warmth of the fireplace.

"'Fraid so, bro." Deke rocked on his boots, not bothering to turn around and look at his younger brother.

Rusty rubbed his hands together, noting the tingle running through them. He knew better than to warm up too fast. That kind of tingle could last for hours. He backed away and let the warmth seep through him, slowly. He ached from sitting the saddle so long, and his muscles had been stretched to the limit using that post hole digger this morning, but he wouldn't complain. He was doing what he loved. Not many men could say that. He had an idea Deke didn't want to hear about how he felt at the moment, either.

Something was on Deke's mind and he instinctively knew he wasn't going to like it from the scowl lining his brother's face. Deke never could hold a poker face.

"Well come on bro, spit it out, I gotta get that post hole digger back to town before noon."

Deke turned slowly to eye his brother, his expression grim and Rusty knew it was bad news of some sort. Deke wasn't usually this slow at coming to the point.

Then Rusty spotted the letter lying on the coffee table, as though it had been read a time or two, the way the paper curled at the edges. Oh God, someone died. For one fleeting second, he thought about his brother Jake, who was the Sheriff over in Peaceful, Texas. But surely, not Jake! He was too young and stubborn to die. He thought of his aging father but knew there would be no letter because his father lived here on the ranch. Then who died? Uncle Dan? No, he wouldn't believe it.

"You remember George O'Leary?"

Rusty let out a long-held breath, the relief he felt warmed him, then he tossed the name around in his head and nodded.

"Vaguely."

"He's the one that took your mama to the hospital the night you were born." Deke informed him.

A grim line formed on Rusty's face, a night he wished he could have changed a million times over. "Yeah."

"You may not appreciate him Rusty, but if he hadn't..."

"Yeah, I know the story, Deke." Rusty couldn't hide his frustration from his brother, he knew him too well.

But darn it, he'd have given his own life, to save his mother's, if he'd had a choice.

Deke frowned at him again. "Maybe you do, and maybe, just maybe, you should hear it again."

"I don't need to." Rusty turned away from Deke, his words slurred with emotion. "I know it by heart."

Deke shook his head at his callus attitude.

"If he hadn't taken mother to the hospital when he did, I might not have been here either. If her time hadn't been so early and I hadn't been so healthy, I wouldn't have made it. Dad's always felt indebted to the man because of that night. Why, I'll never know. It took the only woman he ever loved away from him. It was snowing cats and dogs and Dad was nearly five hundred miles away. There's no way he could have been there on time."

Rusty bit his lip, thinking of the vibrant woman that died that night, so he could be born. It was a sore spot. He didn't want to think about that night...the night his mother died. Nor the guilt for living he carried with him every day.

"So? What about him?"

"He's dead."

The words were said on a long sad note as though this hit Deke close to home. Rusty eyed Deke with renewed interest. They hadn't even seen the O'Leary's in several years, so how could this make Deke so sad? It wasn't like they'd been best of friends and kept in touch.

"I'm sorry." He knew he didn't sound it. But just the mention of his mother had him on the defense. All his life he fought the guilt. It should have been him that died. Then he wouldn't have had to witness the loneliness growing in his father year after year.

"Me too. He was a good man."

Cal Travers entered the room, his eyes going from one to the other, his expression grim. Obviously, he had been the one to read and reread the letter, Rusty surmised.

His father's face was a mask of emotions.

"You may not want to hear this Rusty, but I owed the man so much. Not just for that night. He saved my butt a couple of times too. Never once did he ask for a favor. Never once."

Cal said watching Rusty's reactions.

Rusty felt an unease spread across his shoulders, tighten his muscles. Something wasn't right here. He could feel it in his bones, taste it in his mouth, hear it in the silence. "I didn't know him very well, Dad. I mean I was kinda young at the time. It's been a good twenty-six years since that day."

Deke cleared his throat. "Yeah, well, he sure knew you. But we got a bigger problem than that."

Rusty spread his legs apart, as though physically bracing himself for some bad news. It had to be really bad for Deke to be so serious; his oldest brother was usually full of fun.

"Look, I'm really sorry about the fella. I guess he meant more to you and dad than I realized, but I gotta get back to diggin' holes, bro. Life does go on, you know. And we gotta ranch to run."

"It does, but you don't."

The finality of that statement hit Rusty like a blow to an empty stomach. It must be some problem to stop him from finishing the post holes. And the longer it took Deke to spit it out, the tenser, Rusty grew. Deke always was slow about coming to the point. Rusty did his best to be patient. He owed Deke that much. Whatever it was, it had to be a doozie!

Rusty turned to look directly at Deke. "I don't?"

The question hung in the air. "No, there's something else ..."

He knew there would be, but he wanted to stall, knowing from Deke's expression and his dad's reluctance to say much more, this wasn't going to be good news. Somehow this affected him, and he still didn't see the light.

"I gotta feeling you're doing your best not to tell me something. Why don't you spit it out and let's get this over with," Rusty said going into the kitchen for a cup of hot coffee. Coming back to his brother's side he peered over the rim of his cup at him. The coffee warmed his hands. However, Deke's serious expression hadn't changed. Cal's furrowed brows hadn't relaxed. Something definitely was up.

"Alright, you're right of course."

Surely it couldn't be that bad, could it?

Deke kept rocking on his heels. Rusty watched, fascinated to see his oldest brother so uncomfortable, but disturbed by his frown more than anything.

"Jimmy, Mr. O'Leary's son became a dentist out in Arizona."

Rusty sighed with relief, obviously Deke just needed to talk about this with someone and he was elected. That was okay. He'd listened many times.

Deke firmed his lips and continued. "George's daughter Hannah has been gone for a while, but she's back and just laid him to rest. She's probably a couple years younger than you. You met her once when you were a kid. Anyway, Jimmy can't leave his practice, so she's alone, to run the ranch. And Hannah can't handle that spread without some help. I'm sending you to help her."

Somehow this news didn't sound so bad. Rusty had helped many neighbors through the years. Rusty never considered it a big deal. Why was this different? And he had a gut feeling it was, somehow different. But the expression on Deke's face told him there was more to come. Rusty waited, knowing his brother was about to spit it out and not sure if he wanted to hear the rest, because by now he knew he wasn't going to like what Deke was about to say.

Uneasiness blew through the house like a norther in mid-winter.

"Help her?" Rusty's brow shot up, wondering what was about to happen here. The eerie feeling didn't go away. "So? I've helped a few out here and there, how is this different?"

He could feel the tension growing in his gut.

"Please be open minded about what I'm gonna say, Rusty. But we've got to hash it out. So, listen up, until I'm done, then you can have your say."

Rusty nodded. He'd taken orders from Deke most of his life and this time wouldn't be any different. If there was some kind of a problem, he'd just have to deal with it like a man. Being the youngest, meant he had to reinforce his manhood to his brothers many times.

"Jimmy sent a letter telling us all about his father, how hard he worked, and how much he loved the place. It's their home, their inheritance from the old man. The only thing he had to leave them. He said they both owed Hannah. She practically put Jimmy through school single handedly. He said Hannah is trying to make a go of the place now, but she needs help. It seems George had a gambling problem no one knew about, until he died. Hannah is doing everything in her power to hang on to this place. But when she talked to the lawyers, she was taken aback to find out the old man was in debt up to his eyeballs. She found out the ranch was mortgaged. He put the ranch up as collateral for his personal loans. These are loans that weren't paid back. Hannah has been struggling to hang on, but the bank won't lend her any more money, on just her name. You see, she had been sending her father money all that time."

"So, what's the problem? Just loan her some money." Rusty shrugged as though the matter were settled. He moved to get his hat.

"Can't do that." Cal entered the conversation.

Rusty hesitated. He didn't say anything, just glanced over his shoulder at his father.

"In the first place, she wouldn't accept it, that way. She's got too much pride. Besides, we're pretty well mortgaged as it is with that irrigation system and new baler. Anyway, we can help. The bank said if she had collateral, they'd loan her the money."

"Don't tell me, she doesn't have a dime."

"Basically, as far as the bank is concerned, that's it in a nutshell. What money she made went to putting her brother through dental school, but the money she sent to her father, went down the tube, so to speak." Deke turned his gaze on him now. He looked ready to do battle with him. Something Rusty wasn't accustomed to. He loved all his brothers and doing battle with any of them was like cutting off his own hand. "I've already written her," Deke said staring at his brother.

"And just exactly what did you say?" Rusty came up to face Deke, knowing that whatever was in that letter held his fate.

It was Cal's turn to answer and he strode up almost between them "You've got the collateral, Rusty."

For a full minute, Rusty was silent, the words his father spoke finally hit home and his face turned red, he was sure of it.

"Oh now…" Rusty stared at them in disbelief. "If you're talking about what I think you are talking about, back off, Dad. That's all I have. That breeding stock is all I have for a future. I've busted my butt raising them, nurturing them. And now you just want me to hand them over to some...stranger? I can't believe this!" Rusty began rocking on the heel of his boots now. But with another thought he added. "Besides, if she won't take your money, what makes you think she'll take my collateral?"

"She won't, but you're gonna convince her to." He looked long and hard at his brother now. Then shot a glance at his dad who hung his head. For a moment Deke looked unsure of what he was about to say, then he plunged onward. "The way I see it, there's only one way to make this whole thing work."

Rusty saw his father look upward and knew this was what he had been waiting to hear from the moment he walked in the door...this was the real catch to it all.

"If you married her, you'd have an interest in the ranch yourself, it'd be half yours. You'd see that loan was paid one way or another. If I know you, and I do!"

Rusty's eyes widened, as he looked from one to the other. Were they serious? They wanted him to marry a stranger?

"By God, you've gone nuts!" Rusty threw his hat down on the empty chair and paced for a moment. He shook his head when he looked at Deke again. "This sounds right out of the middle ages. Save the ranch. Marry a complete stranger. That's just about the craziest thing I've ever heard you say, Deke. And my breeding stock, too? Are you out of your mind? You of all people know how much time and effort I've put into them. Babying them all the way." Rusty ran a hand through his hair, rustling it. "You're talking about my life—my future! And not only that, you want me to throw it down the drain for a complete stranger."

"Oh, for Pete's sake, get a grip. You wouldn't have to make a big production out of the wedding. Just get it done legal. And you'd be helping her and fulfilling a family obligation at the same time."

"My obligation you mean!" Rusty slowed his temper, seeing exactly where this was all coming from. Since he owed O'Leary, it was his problem, at least that's how they saw this.

"Well, what's so damned hard to understand, Rusty? We've lived all our lives by our family code. The code of a true cowboy. The code of the west so to speak."

"Don't give me that garbage. Cowboy codes were for the last century, not this one. Oh no, you aren't really going to throw that at me, are you?" Rusty blustered. "The code of the West and all that malarky. That all went out with the horse and buggy. Okay, I can appreciate her problems, sympathize with her too. But *marry* her?"

"Marriage probably sounds like too much, I agree, but think about it, it's the only way to ensure your investment, your prize stock to be exact. By marrying her, you'd have an interest in that place yourself, it would be half yours and we know you'd work to make it a success. Otherwise, you loan her the stock to put up as collateral and you don't know how it would turn out." Rusty was still shaking his head. Deke tried another argument. "Look, Rusty, we help our neighbors. Dad taught us that and Dad was obligated to this man, even though it seems you don't feel any at the moment. And this is one you are going to take care of personally. You've been mooning over Jennifer long enough. It's time you woke up, grew up."

"You've asked a lot of things, but this takes the cake, Deke. It's my stock you are talking about, you know I worked my butt off for that investment. It was my future, and you know it. But to marry her, not to mention my name she'll be using. What if she screws up?"

"Then you'll have to stick around long enough to make sure she doesn't. And if I know you it'll never happen."

"I can't believe you'd ask it of me. I don't owe her anything. This is crazy. Get somebody else." He started toward the door again, but his dad's tempered voice stopped him. It was the kind of calm that blows in just before a tornado hit. Rusty recognized the signs.

"Son, I know it sounds like we're asking a lot. But I depended on my men to help me in a crisis. George was there, every time. When Martha's time came, and I was away on business, George dropped his own problems and was there. He stayed with her until I could get there. He drove what must have been 100 miles an hour to get her to the hospital, in knee deep snow. And the man barely knew how to drive much less in snow. He carried her in himself. He stayed with her as long as they'd let him. And he was the first to see your ugly mug make it into this world. Not only that. He was the one that helped me let go of the memories later...and get on with my life afterwards." Cal's voice almost broke, but he turned away for a second, then back to Rusty. "He'd been through it himself and knew what it took. He told me I had four good reasons to go on with life, 'don't mess it up', he said. He was a real friend Rusty, in every sense of the word. People like that don't grow on trees. I never had a better friend than that...And now it's time to do something for him."

"I've heard the story, dad." Rusty's voice lowered a little, with respect. "And I can appreciate the fact that you feel obligated, but this crosses the line of what you ask of a man, dad. This is going too far! This will ruin my life."

"I know it's a lot to ask." Cal's voice broke again, and he almost turned away, but not before Rusty spotted the unshed tear in his father's eyes.

Dammit! Rusty wanted to run, because when his father got emotional, he knew he'd do almost anything for him. He loved him so.

Then glancing at his youngest son Cal smiled sadly. "But she would have asked..."

Rusty hung his head. They were using the most bothersome trick of all...emotions. Rusty couldn't fight emotions. Not with his family, he cared too much!

"Besides, you can get this annulled in six months to a year and no one will be the wiser. Once the loan is secured, and she's making regular payments, you can walk away from it. If you want to..."

"If I'd want to?" Rusty frowned again. "Why should I marry her?  Give me one good reason?"

Deke nodded. "Because marrying her will make you part owner of that land. And I know you. You fight for what's yours. You always have. You'll make a go of it. And you'll be getting something out of the bargain too. Look, I wouldn't ask you to do this without you getting something from the bargain. This way, you both win. It would ensure the success of the place for her, for the rest of her life, and you'd have something in return, land."

After a moment Rusty looked at them both. "Does she know about this grand plan?"

"Yes, and she's as reluctant as you, but it seems her brother has made her see the wisdom of it."

"So why me? Why not Jake?"

"Jake's got a full-time job in Peaceful now, he can't uproot and go. I owe him that much, we all do. You know as well as I he's already sacrificed more than his fair share. I can't ask it of him. Clint's on vacation with Abby as you well know, and very much married now. So, I certainly can't ask it of him. I've got all I can handle right here with my own brood and running this ranch. And Dad's sure in no shape to handle it. He's pretty upset about the whole thing. He feels he should do something. But you are the only one that can help. So, you're elected." Deke declared as though the matter were settled.

"Aw, for crying out loud Deke. This isn't our business. This isn't the dark ages anymore either. Marrying a complete stranger, that's crazy. Why do we have to get involved with everyone's problems? I mean where does it all end?" He knew even before he argued the point that he would do it, but everything within him propelled him to defend his prize breeding stock to the end, not to mention his own freedom.

"Because that's how we are, Rusty. We're Travers. We stand up for what we believe, take care of our own. Look, we're obligated to the man. And that includes you. It's more your place than any to take care of it. Now I don't want to argue the point with you Rusty. It's a family obligation. Understood?"

"No, it's not understood. It's not fair…it's…"

Then seeing his father's frown, he backed off a little. "I don't even know the man, or his daughter. I didn't know him. I don't owe him anything. Mama died that night. Despite what he might have done for her, she died." Rusty's voice took on an unwelcome emotion.

Cal nodded sadly. "No one's aware of that more than me."

Rusty glanced at his dad and saw the sadness, it matched the hole in his own heart.

One thing hit Rusty, would this ease the guilt he'd carried all his life for living?

Deke turned cold blue eyes on his brother that made Rusty feel guilty and ashamed he had reproached him. "You don't owe him? Just your life..."

Those words sliced through Rusty's heart. A debt he needed to face and pay, once and for all, and then maybe he could get on with his own life.

Deke let that statement hang in midair for a second, then continued to explain.

"Face it Rusty, you are a Travers, and Travers live up to their obligations, like it or not. Maybe it is a little old fashioned. Maybe it's stupid. But we do what has to be done. It's one tradition that we will honor, if I have anything to do with it. Dad told him if he ever needed anything to call on him. The man never asked for anything. Even when he knew he was in trouble, he didn't ask. Not when his boy took off for college leaving him shorthanded or when his debts nearly took him under. He managed, alone, without help. Look boy, quit nursing this hurt for Jennifer. Get your nose out of the ground, pick yourself up and take care of what needs taking care of."

"Is this another 'get over Jennifer' routine'?" Rusty scoffed.

"Everything doesn't center around you and your ex-girlfriend Rusty."

Rusty hung his head. He'd over nursed his feelings for Jennifer. It was over a long time ago, he just hadn't faced it. But he certainly didn't want another female clouding his life. In fact, the less he had to do with females the better.

"If you were in my place, would you do it?" He directed the question to Deke.

"If I was you, yes. I know how it has eaten at you, most of your life. And I know…that Mom will be watching and smiling if you do this. So yes, I'd do it, if I were not married, or had the money to take care of it."

Married! Even if it was just on paper, married was married and he didn't want any part of it! He glanced at them both, frowned and said very slowly..."Mom's death has been my cross to bear..."

"It wasn't your fault son," Cal jumped to console him.

Rusty stared into his father's weathered face and suddenly smiled. "Maybe, but maybe this will help ease that strange pain a man lives with when his mother dies giving birth. Okay...dad, I'll do it for her...and me...and you!"

*****

Married! Was that the best Jimmy could come up with? The one time she depended on him to decide and look where it got her—married! And to some red-necked cowboy she'd never even met.

Who in his right mind would ask such a thing of his sister, after she'd supported him through dental college? After all she'd been through; she didn't deserve being auctioned off to the first available cowboy in the state of Texas.

All she needed to save this place she loved so dearly was money. She'd always made it before. But the thought of going back to Vegas was no longer an option. Her days as a showgirl were over, she refused to wear the outlandish outfits they insisted on, and she'd quit her job without notice. She'd never work in Vegas again, Vic had told her…

She looked down at herself and giggled. No one would suspect under all her ugly barren clothing that she had ever been a showgirl. She deliberately dressed in baggy overalls and flannel shirts to disguise what lay beneath. She didn't want the hands getting the wrong idea. She didn't want any man getting the wrong idea. She had enough wrong ideas to last a lifetime. No man would capture her heart again so easily. No man would drool over her sparsely clad body again, if she could help it. She didn't need that. All she needed was this land!

She glanced about the cattle dotted pasture and smiled, if she could only keep it, her dreams would be complete.

A shiver ran through her as the north wind whispered a lonely song in her ear.

If her father had only put the money away that she'd sent home for the past five years, she wouldn't be needing it now. But he hadn't. He squandered it away in gambling debts. At least Jimmy had made it through dental college and was happily married in Phoenix now. She didn't have to worry about anyone but herself—and keeping this ranch. Her mother was buried on this land, and she'd be damned if anyone would take it from her. It was all she had left of the memory and no one was taking it, no one.

Wild remnants of chestnut hair threatened to fall across her face, and she shoved it back under the floppy hat she'd found in the barn. It probably belonged to her father. Wearing it made her feel just a little closer to the man that she had loved so fiercely. She'd known he liked to have a drink after a long day, and poker was his passion. She simply hadn't known how much he liked it.

Her mind wandered to the Travers family. She couldn't place all of them, had only met a few of them once a long time ago. Why Jimmy insisted that this Rusty Travers was the answer to all her problems, she didn't know. Jimmy didn't know them anymore than she did.

She sighed, edging her horse away from a prairie dog hole, she smiled. "Dagger you must be getting old, you didn't even see that hole, did you boy? Looks like your roaming days are about over."

She petted the sleek coat of her favorite horse and smiled a contented smile. "If Rusty Travers can get me a loan, then I can stay here. And I guess even marriage isn't too high a price to pay. As long as it's in name only."

The horse neighed at her words.

"The cowboy doesn't know what he's in for. I'll make him think—married!"

She giggled and galloped home.

## *Chapter Two*

Rusty drove into the O'Leary ranch yard late that cold February night. There were no lights on in the old-fashioned ranch house, no sign of anyone being up. He stared at the place in silent appreciation. Nothing fancy, but very workable, he decided. He got out of the truck and looked around. He should have waited to come in the daylight. He might scare her to death, but the sooner he talked to her, the better. The urgency inside him gnawed in his stomach.

The wind whipped at his bare neck and he adjusted the collar on his jacket.

Getting married seemed all wrong to him, especially under these conditions. Maybe if he could talk to the girl, they could come up with a better solution. Surely, she didn't want to marry him either.

The ranch was big according to what his brother had told him, encompassing prime acreage. He couldn't blame anyone for wanting to hold onto it. He'd do the same given the circumstances.

Even though the house showed signs of wear and tear, and the barn wasn't in the best of shape, it was truly a working ranch, any cowboy could see that.

He was about to turn around and leave for the nearest town when a low voice curled around him, a very unwelcoming voice. The kind of steel-edged voice that curls around your neck and makes your hair stand straight up.

"Get your hands up, mister. And keep them there."

It was a female voice, even though it rattled on a husky note.

"You must be Hannah O'Leary."

"You've got that right, but it doesn't begin to tell me who you are." she said, her voice sounding much like she'd just woken from a deep sleep. It didn't change the fact that her shotgun was pointed at the middle of his back.

"Not a very nice way to greet your intended, is it?" He tried to turn around, but the butt of the gun stabbed him.

"So, you're Rusty Travers?" the voice sounded just a tad shocked.

"That's me, now will you let me turn around, so I can see who I'm talking to?" He growled angrily.

"Not just yet. How do I know you are a Travers? You sneak in here at this time of night, what on earth for? A cowboy with good sense wouldn't do something like that. Got any identification?"

He pointed to his hip pocket with one finger, "In my wallet."

"Take it out, slowly," she urged him with the tip of the gun.

Rusty reached around and pulled out his wallet, handing it to her.

She took the wallet with one hand and held it up to the dim light coming from the screen door. "I can't see well enough out here. But even if you are, why did you sneak in here in the middle of the night?

"'Cause I," he forgot about the gun and turned around. But there was no seeing the dark shadow that loomed before him. All he saw was baggy pants and heavy wool jacket, and a floppy hat and the cold hard metal that was too damned close for comfort.

"'Cause you what?" she asked still pointing the gun.

"Mind if we get rid of the gun. They tend to go off, you know." He pushed the end of the shotgun away from him and put his hands on his hips as though he were facing down some hombre from the old west.

"You still haven't answered my question. Why did you decide to come in the middle of the night, like some snake?" she asked.

They were both mere shadows to each other, Rusty realized as he tried to get a good look at her. There was no moon to highlight the features, only ominous shadows.

"Look, I just got hit in the face with all this today myself, and needless to say I wasn't thinking too straight. I got a late start, and I wanted to get here to talk to you before everyone showed up for our shotgun wedding." He said on a slightly sarcastic note.

"Why you," and before he knew what hit him, she had jumped him, straddled him, knocking him to the ground. He wrestled her like a bear, a bear that bit, and scratched and pinched.

"Hey, hey," he began as he rolled her over and straddled the top of her. Realizing he had the control he relaxed a little as she panted hard.

"Get off me, you big lug," she demanded, her hair spilling out from her hat like a wild animal, and cloud of darkness covering the ground.

"This is no way to start a marriage, Darlin'," he said sardonically trying to get a good look at her, but unable to make her out in the darkness, no matter how close he got.

White teeth flashed at him, but it wasn't a smile he'd bet.

"Don't you Darlin' me, you big galoot. Get off me."

"No ma'am. Not until you settle down and listen for a minute. I take it you are about as happy about this heavenly union as I am." He said with a chuckle.

For a second, she stilled beneath him, and he realized that whatever she was wearing, it was way too big for her, because her flesh was swallowed in it.

"You can say that again. I don't need a man to save me. And if I marry you, it will be in name only." she gritted.

"Granted. I'm glad we have that straight." He said and rose to help her up.

She didn't take his hand. Getting to her feet she backed away from him.

Another woman came around the side of the house, a shotgun in her hand too. Rusty watched her. She was wearing a robe and had her hair up in some sort of towel or something from the looks of it. He'd sure interrupted them both. But she had a good aim on that shotgun, too. "You all right Miss Hannah?" came the southern drawl.

"I'm fine, Josey. I'm sorry we disturbed you. Go on back to bed. I can handle this one."

The woman seemed to stare at Rusty for a full minute then went back the way she had come. "You just give a holler if you need any help, you hear?" She called over her shoulder.

Rusty faced the wildcat again. "Does everyone on this ranch keep their guns ready?"

"Josey is a little over protective of me..." Hannah replied.

"I can see that."

Hannah seemed to consider the guns and Rusty saw her teeth flash in a quick smile. Then she moved in closer. "Look, this is the most asinine thing I've ever been part of. Naturally, you won't have to hang around once we've got it legal, you know," she insisted grabbing her gun and heading for her house as though he were dismissed.

Not likely.

He followed, not liking the easy way she ignored him. Rejecting him first, hit hard. "I'm afraid I've come to stay for a bit." He announced as they neared the porch.

She whirled around almost in his face. "Stay?"

"Yes ma'am." He adjusted his hat.

"But you just said you don't want this anymore than I do. What's to keep you here?"

"You think we might go in the house to talk about this?" Rusty glanced around the sides of the house, then back at her. "I wouldn't want to disturb anyone else, tonight."

"We aren't going anywhere until you explain that statement." She protested, as her hands went to her hips and her legs spread as though she were about to draw a pistol on him.

He scratched his chin. If he played his cards right, he might get out of the whole thing sooner than he thought. "I don't like this any better than you do, believe me. But I gave my word. And... like it or not, I'll marry you. Then we'll go get that loan you need so badly. But I want to make good and damn sure you put the money where it belongs—on the ranch."

He saw her teeth flash again, but she wasn't smiling this time either and he knew her jaw had dropped in a full-blown gasp, even the gun fell now. "You think I'd *cheat* you?"

It sounded silly even to him, but how could he be sure of anything?

Rusty eyed her strangely. He hadn't meant it to sound so much like a slap in the face, but he was more than a little sure that's how she took it. The woman had pride, he liked that. Independent too, and she sure didn't lack for spunk. If she was half as cute as her spirit, they might get through this without killing each other.

"Let's just say I'm protecting my investment." He saw her pride swell. Damned if he didn't like her grit and determination. Still he didn't know this woman, and he wasn't turning her loose with his name to do as she pleased, especially with his prize-winning breeding stock at stake.

"Investment? So that's what this marriage is all about, you're afraid I'll welsh on my end of the deal." She said bitterly. "What could a red-neck like you have, anyway, that would secure a loan of this size?"

"Try prize winning breeding stock. Mine, every one of them. Hand raised. Now you might have a ranch to lose, but I'll have something to lose too, and that gives me the same leverage as you, lady. But you'll still be using my name for credit, and until I know you are using it for the ranch and not something else, I'll stick around. For all I know you might be like your old man."

He'd gone a little too far, he could tell by the way her head jerked in his direction.

She took a step closer. "And just what do you know about my old man?" She started to slap him, but he caught her arm in midair.

It wasn't quite fair to accuse her of such trickery, but she made him mad. He tried to calm himself for a second, taking a deep breath.

"Look, let's start all over, okay?" He pushed her arm down toward her side. "We got off on the wrong foot, and it's probably my fault for coming in the middle of the night."

He eyed her when she stood silently staring at him. "I'm Rusty Travers, I've come to save you, remember?"

She stared long and hard.

"Save me," she almost laughed, then sobered. "Let me get this straight, you're planning on living here?"

"Yes ma'am, I think I am."

What was he doing? Inviting more trouble into his life. She was letting him off the hook. They could get married and he could go home, simple. Why did he insist on complicating his own life with another female? Maybe not that simple. If he lost his breeding stock, he'd be the one starting over. After all, he didn't know her, and he wasn't sure he could trust this story even if Deke did believe every word of it.

Deep down, he'd known he was stuck, he gave Deke his word. And he'd keep it.

"I won't have it!" she stomped her booted heel against the porch and folded her arms over her chest as though that would do any good.

Rusty was tired, and angry and put out with this temperamental mess of a woman. He bent and hauled her over one shoulder and barged into her home like a bulldozer. He ignored the fact that everywhere he touched seemed almost bony, not at all like Jennifer. Good, his mind took notes. Once inside he set her down in the middle of what looked like a living room.

He turned on the lights, after groping for the switch. The furniture was homey, but comfortably worn. Old fashioned was the word that came to mind as his eyes scanned the room. Dollies on the armchairs, an old rocker, a loomed rug, and a well-used fireplace. Then his eyes landed on her. He stopped dead in his tracks.

Was this his intended wife to be? Surely not. She wore the ugliest pair of overalls he'd ever seen, the most faded flannel shirt he'd ever beheld, and that hat was ready for a trash can. Her hair was a mess, falling in bits and pieces around her face and shoulders. She reminded him of a wild colt.

She wore no make-up, but even without it, he saw classic lines of a woman who could fix up pretty well. Her face was slender, belying the body she hid with her clothes. Her eyes were big and a cow-eyed brown, her brows were finely arched and as dark as her hair. Her skin was almost an olive. He wondered what she might look like with the right clothes and a little make-up.

He winced inwardly; she certainly wasn't anything like Jennifer. But truth be known he couldn't make out what she looked like body wise. That outfit hid everything, probably potbellied or thick waisted and unfit. Jennifer worked out constantly and kept her tiny figure in a perfect eight shape. Just the kind of figure a man liked to sink his hands around. But this—he wasn't sure about. Probably best that she wasn't a knock-out. No chance of him falling for her.

Still her face was a complete shock. In a plain sort of way, she was sorta...cute.

Cute! Where had that come from? He didn't need to be thinking about her as cute.

She seemed to be surveying him too. Her eyes went from head to booted heels and came back to rest on his face, slowly. He couldn't help but wonder if he passed inspection.

Angry eyes stared back at him.

Whether she liked what she saw was debatable from that instant frown she wore.

"How many bedrooms do you have here?" He glanced down the long dark hallway.

She gasped then looked around as though she had to consider the question. "Three, why?

"That's enough. I'll take one. I'm really tired?"

He was already headed down the long hallway looking for an obvious place to sleep. She stared after him. Funny he would have sworn she would try to throw him out.

"The last one on the right...." She informed him.

He stopped when he found it and turned to look at her. Her mouth hung open and he chuckled. She was almost cute when she looked that surprised.

"Mind if I take a quick shower and hit the hay, we can talk this out in the morning."

He turned to find the bathroom at the end of the hall. He nodded and bumped it open with his boot. Then he proceeded to close the door behind him. Not that he was the least bit satisfied with leaving it all up in the air another day, but he'd been digging holes all day, and driving most of the night and a cowboy could only handle so much in one day.

***

Half an hour later, Hannah heard the cowboy come out of the bathroom, felt the humidity from the shower, sniffed the heady scent of freshly showered man, and listened as he crept down the hallway to the spare room.

She was shocked to acknowledge he had more than his fair share of good looks. Good looks? He was gorgeous, who was she kidding. She'd never seen a man in better physical shape. She hadn't expected that. But she knew his type well enough. He was nothing more than a red-necked cowboy, and she wanted no part of him. She wanted him out of here, now more than ever.

But how?

It pained her to admit she would owe him more than a certificate with her name on it and a quick goodbye. But she would owe him. And she hated the debt between them already. That alone could make living with him intolerable.

What worried her most, wasn't the debt she would owe, nor the fact that he didn't trust her. What worried her was that she felt some odd attraction for him. She recognized it as such and knew that was nothing but pure trouble.

*****

Rusty tip-toed through the dark hallway to the room he'd picked out. He turned back the covers on the bed and smelled the sunshine. There was a feather down quilt on top the bed, and it reminded him of home. He smiled. He stretched his sore muscled body across it, wondering just how he planned on handling this woman and this situation. He slipped out of everything but his underwear and slipped between the sheets. He'd left his bag of clothes in the truck, and he wasn't about to go after them now. He'd figure this all out, and soon, but tonight, he was simply too tired to worry about it. He flopped around until he found a soft spot.

He tossed and turned trying to get to sleep and regretted it when he realized the springs gave him away.

Still, he had to figure out what he was doing here. He wanted no part of this whole set up and suddenly he was insinuating himself inside the house and into a bedroom without the slightest thought. He must have gone loco, he sighed and closed his eyes.

Nah, he hadn't gone loco, he just needed some rest. He'd be thinking clearly by morning.

He was relatively safe; this Hannah girl wasn't his type at all. She obviously didn't go in for the more feminine side of her own nature. Just as well. Although that wild mane of hair falling about her shoulders and face did take him by surprise, and finding huge brown eyes staring up at him almost innocently was more than he bargained for, but she certainly was no Jennifer.

There wasn't a chance in the world of falling for this gal, he knew that much. Not that she didn't have a few redeeming qualities. Nice full lips, wild and beautiful hair under that dirty old hat, and what secrets was she hiding with those clothes? It didn't matter, his heart was safe. He did like the way she rebelled at the entire idea though. Glad she wasn't keen on the marrying part either. Maybe come morning they could strike some kind of bargain. Maybe he wouldn't have to marry her.

That was a lot of maybes.

He tried to remember what he felt when he was on top of her though. He couldn't. More bone than flesh. Maybe she was a skinny runt with no figure at all. Maybe she wore clothes like she did to hide it.

Probably no curves at all to her, although he thought he felt a slight softness at her breast. Well, he wouldn't be finding out. He wasn't here for that. Even though she was a mystery and he liked unraveling mysteries most of the time.

No one could ever hold a candle to Jennifer and that was that. No use even thinking along those lines. He'd had the best. It'd be a cold day in hell if he ever found anything to come close to comparing to his Jenny girl.

He closed his eyes again and marveled at the comfort of the bed. Maybe he was just too bone tired to know any difference.

# Chapter Three

"The boys and I thought we heard a ruckus in the yard last night." Someone was saying from the kitchen the next morning.

Rusty halted his steps, listening to her reply. He knew it wasn't polite to listen to other's private conversations, but he needed some kind of edge with this lady. Especially if he was gonna marry her and get her a loan.

"Yeah, the Travers fella came in last night."

There seemed to be a slight pause in the cowboy's reaction. "Where'd he go, his truck is still out front."

"He's in the spare bedroom," came the husky voiced woman that oddly sent a tremor through Rusty with shocked surprise.

"Think that's such a good idea, your being here alone."

Rusty felt his own temper barely simmering. Where'd this hayseed cowboy get off making lewd suggestions like that? But then again, maybe he had a right. He listened a little longer than was polite.

The woman seemed totally oblivious to the suggestiveness of the cowboy's statement. "It doesn't matter. He'll be gone before long."

So, she aimed to get rid of him, as much as that idea appealed to Rusty, it also rankled. It should've been his idea, not hers. He'd hadn't received much of a warm welcome and already she was planning on booting him out. Rusty felt his own rebellious nature stirring.

"You still gonna marry him?"

Another long pause, Rusty noted. "I'm not sure yet. We haven't gotten into any details. It's gonna take a little time to work this out, I'm sure."

"You don't have to do this you know. You got options." The cowboy was saying.

For some reason Rusty didn't like that idea either. It was obvious the cowboy doing all the talking was much older than she and somehow it seemed indecent.

"Thanks Burt, but you don't have that kind of money, nor credit." She turned him down flat. Although turning him down for the obvious reasons seemed more natural to Rusty. Maybe she liked older men, a father image.

"I've been saving. I've got enough for a small spread..."

Rusty burst into the room then and she sloshed half her coffee on her hand. It burned, and the older cowboy took her to the sink immediately to wash it off and help her. The intimate way he was holding her hand and the expression on his face told Rusty he was either already in her life or trying to insinuate himself very quickly. For some reason it rubbed Rusty raw. He was too old.

"Good morning." Rusty tried to sound chipper.

The frown was in place on Hannah's face as she turned to look at him. "Good morning, this is my foreman, Burt Stockton."

"Burt ..." Rusty nodded, his gaze flitting over the cowboy with quick appraisal.

Was she trying to explain who the man was, or who he was to her? Rusty almost smiled.

It seemed pretty plain that whatever he thought of her, she didn't reciprocate, but still the old man persisted.

"Mind if I help myself to the coffee, ma'am?" Rusty asked trying to stay out of their way.

"No, go ahead," she said pushing away from the older cowboy and moving toward the table with her mug again.

"I better git."

"Later, Burt," she called after him.

"Nice fella." Rusty's smirk hadn't escaped her.

"Yes, he is," she affirmed with another frown in place again, as though she wore it just for him. "He's worked here all my life. My dad hired him twenty years ago, and he's been here ever since. Anything you need to know about the ranch, you can ask Burt."

He hated to see the frown back in place, because he suddenly realized he liked her crooked kind of smile.

"Maybe it's none of my business, or maybe I shouldn't ask but ..."

"There's nothing between Burt and me, if that's what you're thinking."

Rusty nodded. "If you say so."

She seemed to brace herself for conflict. "Look, let's get something straight here. What's about to happen, isn't personal either."

"You mean us getting married."

"That's right. Don't think for one minute I don't know why you want to marry me. I'm fully aware that Texas is a community property state and that your 'investment' would be protected. So, don't pretend this is charity. By my agreeing to this so-called marriage, we become partners. It's the only thing, oddly enough, that makes any sense to me."

"What? Us getting married?"

"No, being partners, sharing the load, so to speak."

"Glad you cleared that up. I guess we understand each other pretty well, then." Rusty smiled again. He liked her spunk and her direct approach to any subject. It made him think he might trust her.

"Good. And as such I expect you to work just as hard if not harder than the rest. After all, you'll have an interest to look out for, won't you?" she got up and went toward the old gas stove. It was a bare kitchen floor and cold obviously from the way she ran around in her socks. She was in the middle of cooking from the looks of it. The eggs were light and fluffy and Rusty's mouth was already watering. Obviously, the woman could cook.

Rusty swallowed her words with silent agreement. She was right, what could he say?

"Hungry?" She asked when his eyes never left the frying pan.

"Do ducks quack?" He smiled.

That got a real smile out of her and he was stunned at the difference a smile made on Hannah's face. Like lighting a candle, the glow was magnificent. It made her eyes bigger, her mouth fuller, more sensual. He cleared his throat and cast his glance back on the eggs.

She served him a large helping of eggs and added a couple of strips of bacon and a couple of biscuits. He reached for a couple more.

She almost smiled again, as she set the jelly on the table. It was home-made strawberry and he couldn't wait to try it. But her open stare made him chuckle.

He glanced at her apologetically. "Sorry, I've been digging post holes this week and can't stay out of the kitchen."

"That's hard work, especially in the winter. The ground is so hard; it doesn't co-operate with muscle at all." she acknowledged. "A man needs good food when he's working hard."

Her glance drifted to his shoulders and back, then back to his face.

He dug into the eggs. "Yes ma'am."

She leaned back in her chair, her arm stretched over the back of it. She was dressed a little better this morning. She wore overalls, but the shirt was a pretty yellow and her hair was shining as though she'd just stepped out of the shower. She must have used some fancy soap too, because she smelled like a fresh flower garden.

Of course, he wasn't looking at her like a woman, really, or even thinking along those lines. He couldn't allow himself to get carried away with a situation that would only be temporary. Besides, Hannah wasn't his type. There would be no ties when he left. If he gauged her right, she felt the same. At least she was a sensible woman.

He gobbled his food quickly.

"You're a good cook," he said when he noticed her staring

"Have to be, to feed this crew."

"How many you got?"

"Ten. They all worked for my father." She added as though that made any difference to him.

"Maybe you ought to let a couple go, to save a little." He suggested. "Don't need as many hands in the winter..."

Something she didn't like, he quickly realized when she bit her lower lip and frowned again.

"I think it's time we got a few things straight around here." Her voice was laced with a bitter edge now, as though the welcome wagon was no longer extended.

Obviously, she was about to set him straight on just who ran this place...her!

Rusty knew what was coming. He found talking to her like a man. She even reacted like one, at least a rancher.

"You fixing to put me in my place?" He lowered his voice and leaned toward her.

"That's right. And the first thing is, my hands stay. All of them. They've lived here for years. In the winter, they all pitch in do what needs to be done, take little pay and work as though they owned the place. They've been here all my life, most of them, and I won't get rid of them. Not one. That's already been decided, by me! Understood?"

"Understood. But I have a few suggestions that in the long run would save you a little. If you care about these hands, and they've been faithful workers for so many years, you should consider giving them a small piece of the land. As I hear it, you've got enough. That black woman with the shotgun, I take it, she cooks for the bunch, and you don't need her...Not the way you cook."

"I beg your pardon." Now she was mad. Her cheeks were pink and her eyes sparkling with a life of their own. "I certainly do need her. She's..." She stopped for a minute obviously wondering how he knew what Josey did around here.

"No ma'am. You cook well enough to serve the men here. You could give them some land and retire her except on special occasions."

"I will not retire her. She's not a cow to be pastured. She's human. She'd think she wasn't needed. No, I won't do that. Josey is family. Besides, I don't have time to cook for the men; I'm a rancher, in case you hadn't noticed. That means I get out there with the best of them and put in a full day's work."

Rusty shook his head. "I figured as much." Rusty would take this subject up later. Maybe it was too soon to offer advice. From the look on her face, she didn't want his opinions. Not yet, anyway. "Now," He adjusted his hat and eyed her, "exactly where is my place?"

"This whole scheme was your brother's and my brother's idea." She waited for him to nod. "Not mine. Nor yours, I'm thinking. The only reason I'm vaguely considering it is because I don't want to lose my home. It means too much to me. This is my home, it's been my home all my life. No matter where I go, this is always home. For more reasons than I want to go into. I won't lose it. If you have the collateral, I don't see why we don't just go get the loan and you can be on your way. However, this marriage scheme seems to be the way you are insuring the loan is paid and you get something for your trouble. I respect and understand that as a business woman. Since it will make you part owner of the Double Bow Ranch."

Rusty wiped his mouth and sat back in the chair for a minute to really give her a look. "I've got the collateral, that's true enough. And that collateral you keep referring to...is my future….my only future. A man doesn't just give away his future without some insurance." He hesitated to let that soak in for a minute. "But there's a problem. I don't know you, lady. I don't know if I can trust you to do the right thing or not. And I'm not turning my entire future over to a stranger to do with as they please. If I'm gonna invest in this loan, I'll be a part of it."

He let that bit of news hit her between the eyes, as he continued. "I'm putting up State Champion Breeding stock, that's my lifetime investment. I'm losing everything because you need this loan. The way I see it, marriage is the only thing that will compensate me for any of it. Sure, it will make me a part owner, and rightfully so. But I can guarantee you it would be better than a bank owning it. I work for what I get, and this ranch would be no different."

"I appreciate your honesty. But you have to see my point too." She frowned. "I don't take marriage lightly."

Rusty studied her intently. "Look, once we are married this ranch is half mine. Then the odds even out some. We'll both have something to fight for. I'm a Travers, and even though that might not mean much to you. We Travers fight for what's ours. And we'll fight for it together." Rusty took in a long breath, realizing he had just consented to his brother's crazy scheme. "So, you see you'll be gaining something else in this bargain, a partner who will fight as hard and as long as needed to see it succeeds."

She seemed to study his words for a moment, her expression growing more thoughtful, less angry. "I've read about your breeding stock. Quite impressive." She hesitated again and gazed into his eyes, the sincerity holding his attention. "And... granted, you would be risking something of great value. Even I realize that. If the positions were reversed, I might feel the same as you. It's just that getting married seems so extreme."

She waited for his nod again. It was slow in coming.

"Just so you know that I've made some efforts on my own. I've applied for a loan. They turned me down the first time, but I've asked for reconsideration. Let's go into town and see what they say before we jump the gun, okay?" She suggested, putting her hat on her head and glancing at him to see if he was through eating. "Could be the matter will be settled for us."

Rusty grabbed one more bite of biscuit and nodded. But he had many dealings with banks and he knew she was in for a big disappointment. Banks didn't deal with sentiments. They dealt with cold hard cash. Still, he admired her grit. He'd see her through this. Then be on his way. "I'm right behind you."

He offered to drive her into town in his truck, but she refused, insisting on her rattle trap of a Ford pickup. It had no heat, no radio, and it was obviously a work truck. It had certainly been banged around.

She didn't apologize for the chug holes either, nor the lack of springs on the truck. He bounced all the way to town, feeling more like the jeans in the dryer than a man about to save a little gal from the big bad banker.

"You make a mean breakfast lady, where'd you learn to cook?" Rusty wanted to take the edge off her testiness.

"My daddy taught me a lot, and Josey taught me some. I enjoy cooking when I have the time. If we do manage to secure the loan, I will consider what you said about Josey's retirement. Could be, she is waiting for something like that. She deserves a retirement if anyone does. She's been working here so long though, I'd have to use some tact on how I introduced it to her. And giving her a small piece of land would really make that retirement worthwhile. I wonder why I never thought of it?"

He eyed her closely wondering why she actually considered anything he had said so far. She didn't seem the type to give in to anyone else's opinion so easily. Rusty glanced at her sideways, trying to put all the pieces of the puzzle together. Nothing seemed to fit with Hannah, though. She was a surprise in every direction. Admitting he was right must have taken some courage. The lady had grit.

As they pulled into the parking space, she headed straight for the bank, and never once looked back to see if he was following her.

He was right behind her all the way, swinging the bank door closed behind them.

Unlike Jennifer she didn't wait for him to open the door for her or act as though she thought about it. She did for herself. In some ways he liked that, in other ways it brought out the rebel in him, making him want to put her in her place. If she had a place, that is!

But Hannah was no regular female. He'd known that right from the beginning. She hadn't even changed clothes to come to town. She was a rancher through and through and all business.

A big burly man, with thick silver hair, and ruddy complexion came out of the inner office and glanced at her. His glance alone spoke volumes. For an instant his faced flashed red, frustration lining his weathered brow. He was a closed book, Rusty decided quickly. The man started to turn away after he saw her, but she flagged him down. "Mr. Simmons, I've come about the loan."

Mr. Simmons seemed to stop short, his stature swelling with obvious frustration, he glanced at her again, paused, sighed and then looked at Rusty, obviously trying to place him and coming up blank.

"Step this way, won't you?"

Rusty could see the answer on the man's face before she ever opened her mouth. He was not going to even consider the loan. This was going to be like arguing with a wall. And for a brief moment, Rusty wanted to argue her case for her.

Just because she was a woman didn't mean she didn't deserve some respect. Where he came from, women got it whether they deserved it or not.

"I'm sorry; Miss O'Leary, but I can't do it. I've put it before the board, and they all agree. Our hands are tied. If you had collateral, more credit, something." He closed the door behind them.

Rusty saw her back straighten, her nose lift, and her anger rise. He saw her brow lifting with what could only be called solid determination as she faced the man that refused to argue her case.

Damn he liked her grit.

"Mr. Simmons," she said, getting right up in his face, forcing the man to not only look straight at her, but listen as well. "You know very well I helped put my brother through dental school. Doesn't that speak for something?" Her voice didn't quiver or shake. She was nearly as bull headed as himself and darned if Rusty didn't like every inch of that. He knew it took all her courage not to shout or cry. Her expression was hot, and still very determined, as though she might actually win the battle with this stubborn man. "I mean there was a time when a person's reputation spoke for itself."

"It speaks highly of you, yes. And as an individual yes. And I'll admit I admire you, admire your tenacity, but that doesn't pay for loans."

Mr. Simmons seemed to sense her retaliation before she spoke. He held up a hand. "Your father didn't put his money in this bank. In any bank. He squandered it. I'm afraid. I feel for you, truly, but there is nothing I can do. We have policies we have to go by. Rules."

"Granted dad made some bad decisions. But...he loved the place. His wife...my mother is buried there. He'd never risk losing it..."

"It appears he did risk it!" The man paused to give her a moment's consideration. Then he added, sincerely. "I'm sorry. I've done all I can do." He was shaking his head and doing his best to dismiss her, Rusty concluded with a building anger himself.

"Can't you see I'm trying?" She didn't hesitate to inform him. "Doesn't that say something for my character? Use to a man's word was enough."

"Yes, that's very true. It was." The man paused again to give her a slight smile. "But I'm afraid that banks these days don't do business on character alone."

Rusty took this information in with grim silence. The woman made money somewhere besides the ranch, and he wondered exactly what she had done for a living. It made him see how much he didn't know about her. However, there was quality in Hannah that had to be admired. She was stubborn, hard to deal with, and yet, she was willing to do almost anything for that ranch she called home. He respected that. Admired it, understood it. And he began to trust.

"It's sad, but maybe if you'd have returned and checked on the money, you would have seen what he was doing. Maybe you could go back to your job and pay for it, that way."

"I couldn't do that." Hannah visibly shuddered. "But I'll get the money."

He glanced at Rusty then her, "Well, until you do there's nothing I can do. I've told you this already. The subject is closed. You have until the fifteenth of next month. After that, it's totally out of my hands."

Without a second thought Rusty stood up and glared at the banker. "Well there's something I can do."

Dammit, he had a little of Deke in him, he reckoned for getting himself into something too deep. But he was here now, and he saw the problem and darned if he didn't half agree with his brother. The girl had enough gumption to support her father and her brother and no one seemed to be giving her any due for it. It wasn't fair! Someone had to fight for the underdog, and Hannah was definitely the underdog.

Hannah started to open her mouth, but he raised his hand and looked at her. "The name's Rusty Travers and I'm moving my account here, to your bank. I'm also engaged to this lady, so mind how you talk to her."

"Engaged? Travers? Sounds a little familiar but I'm not sure where I've heard of you. I don't see that has anything to do with me."

"I'm sure you don't. But you will, sir, you will." Rusty said and grabbed Hannah's arm and stalked out of the building.

He was totally unaware of holding Hannah's arm until they reached the truck. Why he had gotten so riled he wasn't sure, but if business was done like this, no one would have come west so many years ago.

He didn't notice the heat that seemed to rise between them, nor the frown on her face when she realized he had practically marched her out of the bank and onto the street. He was too keyed up himself.

"Did you have to act like that?" She spat, pulling away from him and starting for the driver's side of the truck. He pushed past her and opened the door, then got in himself.

She stared at him, "That's my truck!"

"Yes ma'am, but I won't be bounced from here to yonder again. Now get in." He demanded in no uncertain terms.

She opened her mouth to protest, but something in his expression stopped her.

Wise woman!

They rode in silence for a long spell before he broke it. Then suddenly he pulled off to the side of the road. He jerked the truck into park and turned to look at her.

"Okay, let's talk."

He saw the frown, lined with disappointment she had been hiding. It nearly broke his heart to have to yell at a woman who'd been so wronged by a bank manager. The cold hard facts about banking was that they dealt in money and that's all there was to it.

"You need a loan; they won't give it to you. I've got the collateral to get that loan. Your problems are over Hannah."

Hannah seemed to consider his words. He could tell it nagged at her to accept his help. He even understood that kind of pride.

"Or just beginning." She glanced at him hard.

"I know getting married to a total stranger doesn't appeal to you any more than it does to me, but at least this way, we both win. And we go into the situation honestly." He questioned. "Now how much do you owe?"

"$97,000 now, the same in six months." She said. Rusty whistled through his teeth.

"Damn!" He countered, pushing his hat back from his face.

"I guess, putting up your cattle is a very hard thing to do. It certainly would be for me. No, if it were me, I'm not sure I'd do it." She stilled a moment. "If you want to pull out of this whole deal, I'll understand." She countered.

"I've got A1 credit, stocks, bonds..."

She shook her head and turned to look away, as though her pride needed a readjustment. "Look, I appreciate what you are saying. Really, I do. But unless you use the collateral you have, it just won't hold water. But I think getting married is going just a little too far. Don't you?"

For some unknown reason, Rusty reached across and pulled her chin around, just in time to see one tear fall against a cheek that was surprisingly soft. He cleared his throat and backed away again, removing his fingers from her chin, that quivered. This woman's behavior had him rattled. She was soft one moment and hard as nails the next.

"You just want to give up, then?" He asked gruffly. She hesitated.

He didn't see this woman giving up anything. She was a fighter, he could feel it.

"No... but I don't see—"

"We'll get married, I'll hang around long enough to make sure things are going okay… A lot of things can go wrong on a ranch, Hannah. I'm sure you know that as well as I do. Things you can't control. Bad weather, unhealthy stock, freak disasters. I'm not just marrying you for half the ranch. I have a home to go to. But putting up my stock means getting involved and if I get involved, I want to stick around and make sure everything is going to be okay, too. With two of us trying it will make things easier. I'll have as much to lose or more than you, this way. Besides, I'm really not the bad guy here." Rusty stated, gripping the steering wheel tighter. "I've got the good credit, the collateral, and by golly they will listen up when we are married. Think of the marriage as insurance. With my name your credit will improve, and you'll be able to save further disasters down the road. When I'm long gone. You may not know me, like me, or think much of me, but once we are married you will be a Travers, and by golly that's a name to be proud of."

Again, she was silent. He felt her resistance and wondered why she was so against marriage. Had someone hurt her? Did she love that Burt fella? None of the answers he conjured made him feel any better.

"Deal?" he asked when she said no more.

"Deal." she let out a long-held breath. "But," she hesitated and stared him down again. "I hope you realize that this isn't going to be a real marriage. I mean, I'm not..."

"You're setting the terms for that one, lady," he smiled as he started the truck again and headed for her ranch. "The way I see it, that's the least of our worries right now."

# Chapter Four

They were nearly home when a strange looking dog ran out in front of the truck and Rusty slammed on the brakes. The dog had been limping, and now lay panting against the cold and lonely stretch of highway.

Rusty got out, slammed his door and went to check on it. Hannah followed him.

"Is he dying?" she asked in a suddenly choked voice.

Rusty raised up and looked into big pools of tearful eyes. He couldn't quite believe this woman sometimes. Hard as nails, most of the time. He guessed she really did have ranching in the blood.

From the time he was a little scamp he knew that animals were important to maintaining a ranch, all animals. But his love of dogs had been different, he never saw them as working animals, only as pets.

He shook his head, and turned back to the dog, not wanting her to see the admiration in his face. It wouldn't do for her to think he liked her. So, he bent to the task of taking care of the dog.

The dog whimpered when Rusty picked him up and placed him in the back of the truck.

Hannah didn't say a word, just got into the truck and waited.

"Where's the closest vet?" He cast her a curious glance.

"Couple of miles down the road on the right. Doc Ferguson usually takes care of my stock."

"Good, just point the way," Rusty said pulling back onto the highway and chancing a look at the distress on Hannah's face.

She held her tears well, but she was shaking, and he knew she was about to fall apart on him. Just what he needed. Who'd have thought his hard-hearted Hannah would deep down have a heart of mush?

He drove a little faster.

The vet was busy, but when they pulled up with such speed into the drive, he ran out to check on them. Rusty eyed the man closely, a short, heavyset man in his fifties with a somber face and a gentle look about him.

"Got a hurt dog, here," Rusty explained.

"A dog you say?" The doc didn't waste any time as Rusty led him to him.

Hannah hung onto the truck bed and stared at the bleeding animal.

"Your dog, Hannah?" the doc asked as he meticulously handled the animal with care.

"No, he was crossing the road."

"Haven't seen this one around. You gonna take care of his bill?" the doc asked Rusty over his thin rimmed glasses.

Rusty nodded.

An hour later the dog was patched. Rusty put him back in the truck and continued on as though nothing had happened. Only something had. Hannah hadn't said a word during that hour. It was as though she'd been holding her breath.

When they reached the ranch Rusty made a bed for the dog in the barn and Hannah carried food scraps and water to him. She tried to act as though the dog's affectionate licks weren't appreciated, but Rusty saw the gleam in her eyes.

"Gonna keep him?" Rusty asked eyeing her closely.

"I don't know," Hannah answered, as she cradled the dog's head. "You paid his bill. The way I see it, he's yours."

Rusty considered her words. "Okay, but he'll have to stay here, at your ranch."

He noticed that calling it 'her' ranch lifted her shoulders some and made her almost smile again. "I guess, for a while, is alright. His owner might show up. If he has an owner. He's a real mutt." She absently scratched behind the dog's ears, and the dog's tail began to thump.

"Mutt's make the best pets," Rusty laughed.

"Pet?"

"Sure, haven't you had a pet before?" He teased.

"No." Hannah's face pinked. "I mean...not really a pet."

"Why not?"

"Animals are for work on a ranch, not for pets." Hannah explained. "My dad taught me a long time ago there wasn't room on a ranch for pets. Attachments like that just lead to heartache."

"Well, we got ourselves a pet now." He thought about what she said and added, "Besides, sometimes life is worth a few heartaches."

Hannah smiled again, and Rusty found himself warming to that smile for he knew it was sincere.

He pulled her up, and for a split second their eyes met and held. Some strange feeling flushed through Rusty, but he scoffed at it. It was only compassion...not passion.

He was about to talk to her about the wedding arrangements, when Burt walked up, and she turned all her attention to him and the problems he'd brought to her. It seemed to Rusty as though this Burt fella was around a lot, and always with one problem or another.

Rusty felt a pang of regret. For a minute there, he thought he might take a real liking to Hannah. But that wasn't good thinking. No use getting his emotions involved. This would only be a marriage in name. No use even thinking in any other direction. Besides, he knew he'd be measuring her against Jennifer, and frankly the two were not in the same league.

It dawned on him that maybe Burt could help her, and he could be on his way. However, she would never be happy with another ranch, that was a done deal. So, good ole Burt was gonna have to share his "woman".

Rusty wandered about the ranch most of the day, meeting the boys in the bunkhouse, getting used to the lay of the land. Jose was the oldest and seemed almost eager to show him about and introduce him. Then he met Cully, Slim and Pete, all veteran ranch hands, and seemed to identify with him immediately. A couple of younger wranglers kept to themselves. Then there were several Mexican hands that Jose had brought to the ranch from the old country. And one big black man. He was bigger than most of them put together, and obviously married to Josey.

He met Josey on several occasions as she went back and forth between the ranch house and the bunk house. Rusty noted the way Josey seemed to "Mama" Hannah, and eye him suspiciously. If he could gain her trust, Hannah might start listening to him.

"You don't look like you trust me, Josey." Rusty remarked when she stood staring at him from the screen door of the ranch house the next morning.

"Not yet, I don't. I'll have my eye on you, and you better treat Miss Hannah right, or you'll have me to answer to, understand?"

"Yes, ma'am." Rusty tipped his hat to the woman and headed out to the pasture. It was a cold gray morning, the kind that made a man want to stay in bed and snuggle into the covers. But those days were gone. He was a man now and responsibilities had him facing the world head on. Even Hannah.

It seemed Josey was hanging about a lot. He was sure Hannah was reluctant to be alone with him, and Josey knew it. Maybe in Hannah's shoes, he'd feel the same way.

As evening grew near and he found himself restless and displaced. He'd managed a full day's work, what with feeding the bulls and poor stock, and checking the watering holes for ice. Jose and Cully riding alongside him most of the day, pointing out the lay of the land. He didn't belong here even though the boys in the bunkhouse did everything to make him feel at home. They soon recognized he was an experienced rancher. Rusty thought about the men and how most of them seemed to respond to his light instructions upon one or two occasions throughout the day. No one balked. One thing a real cowboy recognized was experience. And Rusty was full of experience, thanks to Deke.

The next day was the same. He broke sweat that day even though the temperature only climbed to the low 30's, wrangling strays out of brambles, mustering the cattle together, and checking fence lines. He missed the trees, there just weren't many here and what little there were seem scrawny.

Rusty knew he hadn't been completely accepted yet. He wondered if Burt had anything to do with that. It was obvious that Rusty had taken Burt's position, a fact that Burt didn't cotton to. Not that Rusty blamed the man entirely, but if he really cared so much for Hannah surely, he'd see it was for her own good.

"Supper's ready," Hannah said in a husky voice as she found him in the barn a few evenings later. He'd been taking his meals in the bunkhouse and waiting until Hannah retired to go in the house. This day was especially cold and Rusty hankered for home and hearth. He was in the middle of feeling sorry for himself, cleaning a stall as the evening dust settled.

He'd never been homesick in his life, until now. But the feeling of not really belonging ate at him.

"Thanks, I'm a little hungry," he grinned, surprised to know he was actually invited to the ranch house to eat. He didn't mind eating in the bunkhouse, Josey was a great cook, but with Burt's ever prying eyes pinned on him most of the time, he didn't look forward to it. Usually Cully and Jose would get him involved in a poker game, but he wasn't in the mood this evening.

"You've done a full day's work." She smiled again, and damned if Rusty's insides didn't heat up. Whoa boy, this one wasn't his type and there was no reason to even think along those lines.

They walked in silence to the house. Rusty pondered that quick flash of reaction. Then doused it, as just a tired cowboy, lonesome for home.

It startled him to find no one at the table but himself and her. He wondered if she ate alone every night. Not even Josey joined her. He wondered at that. Hannah was such a puzzle, not like any woman he'd known. Of course, the only woman he'd really known much of was Jennifer and she was not solitary in anything she did.

"Hope you like Chicken Fried Steak and gravy." She said serving him moments later as though it were a natural thing to do.

"Yes ma'am. I was just wondering why Ms. Josey doesn't join you in the evenings."

"Josey lives in a small house down by the creek. It used to be a line shack, but we don't use it anymore."

"I see."

Rusty marveled at how Hannah had worked right alongside him most of the day, not once counter- minding his orders, and now, she had fixed supper for him. The woman was a worker, and a mystery.

"This sure looks good." Rusty licked his lips and glanced at the Texas size steak and smooth cream gravy she served up.

She seemed to note the action and blushed. Either Hannah didn't get many compliments, or she was downright shy about them, Rusty decided. Well, she'd get a few from him, if this kind of cooking continued. One thing any cowboy appreciated was a good meal.

She'd combed her hair, but she still wore the old clothes and he couldn't keep his mouth closed about it. Most of the females he knew were constantly primping, so what was her problem? Even if they didn't wear dresses, most of them wore tight fitting jeans, and well fitted t-shirts. Not Hannah though.

She noticed the way he kept staring at her attire and reddened, then hastened to explain. "I'm a rancher, we don't have time for frills around here."

"Yes ma'am." Minutes passed without a word of conversation between them. Then he opened his mouth and put his foot in it.

"But you do dress up on occasion I take it." He didn't look at her.

She glanced down at herself and shrugged. She didn't even look at him when she spoke. "Not very often. This is a working ranch, Mr. Travers, not a dude ranch. And what I wear has nothing to do with you."

"Call me Rusty, ma'am, and yes ma'am, I can see that. Guess I'm just not used to too many ranching women."

Still even his sisters-in-law wore dresses every now and then.

He wondered if she'd even wear a dress when they were married.

That thought woke him up. What was he doing wondering about her state of dress? She was nothing to him. It didn't matter if she wanted to wear overalls to her wedding, he wouldn't say a word. This was not going to be a match made in heaven and he knew better than to go there. But the curiosity that her clothes caused him great distress made him uncomfortable. It was just a little hard thinking of her as a cowboy and not a woman. After all, she had beautiful hands and fingernails, always clean and polished. She had the fullest, deepest pink lips he had ever seen, and his imagination wandered there too often to count.

"I think we should talk about the wedding, don't you?" He asked as he finished off the steak and potatoes with a satisfied sigh. He wasn't in anymore a mood to talk about the wedding than she, but once things were settled maybe they could both relax a little.

"I guess so—" Enthusiastic she wasn't!

"Have you ever been married?" he asked as casually as he could.

"No!" she answered harshly. Then cast him a frown. "Have you?"

"Nope."

He cleared his throat wondering how he was gonna have this conversation without making her just a tad mad. The lady wasn't in the market for a husband that was for sure. That suited him fine, except...most women considered him a pretty good catch. Most women—not Hannah.

"This being your first time and all, do you want a wedding or..."

"No..." she protested vehemently. She stood up from the table and paced a little, trying to find something to busy herself with. She was more than a little uncomfortable with this conversation and he wished he hadn't started it. But he had. "I'd say a quick Justice of the Peace should do just fine, how about you?"

Justice of the Peace, his mind yelled back at him! Dang it! He didn't like it. Now that he thought of it. Not one Travers had ever been married by anything less than a full-fledged preacher and he suddenly felt cheated. A judge just wasn't the same. It seemed unholy. It seemed sacrilegious. Didn't she want a wedding, with her neighbors around, and a pretty white dress?

Then something hit him that made his insides hot. Was she a virgin? From the looks of her, he'd guess she was. What man would court her, looking like she did? Not so much her, but the clothes. A cold approach to their wedding was so unexpected, he wasn't so sure. Maybe she wasn't. Maybe she was ...

He had to stop thinking about things like that. Where had it come from? Jennifer was the only girl he'd ever cared about that way and he wasn't about to go thinking about Hannah romantically.

She'd set the rules, he'd abide.

"I'd prefer a preacher." he heard himself say. He could have ripped his own tongue out. What had gotten into him? She was completely right about this, very practical. Just what he should be appreciating about her. But he wasn't. So, what had gotten into him?

"A preacher?" she said indignantly, as she leaned against the counter, folding her arms over her breast, a frown lining her face.

She stammered and stuttered and flounced about the room like a wild animal one minute, then would stop and stare at him the next. "Next thing you know, you'll want a full-fledged wedding."

"Something wrong with that?" He heard himself ask. "We've got to be believed. Even though this is a marriage in name only, we've got to convince the community we are in love and want this marriage. Hannah quit thinking of this as some kind of trap. This is business. This ranch isn't going to save itself. You are going to have to turn a profit to stand on your feet. I'm going to help you do just that. But it will take time and lots of hard work."

"I'm not afraid of hard work. But it's a little hard to separate business and marriage though." she gasped. "You can't be serious. Where in the world did word love come from, this has nothing to do with love. You're here to help me save this ranch, and that's all you're here for, got it? And if you think we can fool everyone, you're crazy. I've lived here all my life. People know me."

"I got it. But I damned sure am, serious." He fired right back at her. "That banker gets the idea that I'm here today and gone tomorrow, you won't get that credit, no matter what. We can't just get married one day and annul it the next. He's no dummy. It's all a game, Hannah. You have to play the game if you want the credit. They have to think of us as an outstanding couple in the community, someone that's gonna be here tomorrow. If he suspicions, I'm just here to get that loan for you and won't be sticking around, he won't give it to us. He'll still consider you a risk. If he sees that I'm half owner he's gonna respect that and expect me to be here to see it is taken care of. Which is only right."

"I don't care what he thinks, what anyone thinks. Once you put the stock up, how can they possibly refuse us the loan?"

"They won't refuse it. That's not the entire picture Hannah. Getting the loan is the first step, but it doesn't solve all the problems. Even with a new loan, the money has to be paid on time. Whether there's a drought and we lose cattle, whether we get sick and can't take care of the place. All kinds of things happen. That's why I'm here. You aren't gonna lose this place if I can help it. The odds are better if two of us are running things around here. You've got good hands Hannah, but they don't run the place. There isn't a one of them that is a leader. Not even good ole Burt."

"Well...maybe..."

"And oh yes you do care. You don't want a wedding because it isn't gonna be a real marriage. That means you do care. And you want that loan approved, more than anything I'm guessing, or you wouldn't be agreeing to this...wedding."

She stared at him in disbelief. As though he had two heads. As though what he said made her angry. Why was she angry? Most girls would insist on a wedding. What was wrong with her? Especially if she'd never...

There he went again, thinking about things he shouldn't be thinking about.

"We aren't in love and no one's going to believe we are—"

"Don't be so sure. All brides are bashful...at first. Naturally, I can't just marry you. That would be too obvious. I can't just pop up out of nowhere, and get the loan taken care of. We have to do this right. So, we'll allow some time, for a courtship. We told the banker we were engaged. That's enough for now. But we'll be married before the fifteenth of next month and we'll get that credit. You wait and see. People will say, 'There goes Hannah's man.'"

"What are you talking about...courtship?"

"A courtship."

She looked at him dumbfounded then broke out in a laugh. "That's the most ridiculous thing I've ever heard."

"No—it isn't. Clint courted Abby right back into his life. Besides, it makes sense. I can't just pop up out of nowhere and suddenly claim you. No one would believe it. Everyone would wonder where I came from and when I was leaving. We need to give it time. I got the time if you do. We have to do this right Hannah or there's no use doing it at all. That banker wants collateral. I've got it. Even though you don't cotton to marrying me, if I do, I'll have a greater interest in the ranch myself. I'll have more of a reason to make sure those payments are made on time…"

"Well I don't have time for games. And who is Clint and Abby?"

"We've got to take this seriously if we want others to believe us. And Clint is my brother, one of them. Abby was our neighbor. Now she's Clint's wife. Look, I know you don't particularly cotton to me, but we've got to convince some of the people around here that we're in love and gonna get married. That way, they won't suspect it's a ploy to obtain the loan. And when the time comes, you can just say I left you for another woman."

"Left me for another woman?" She reeled on him now, as though that were an important issue. Now he'd set her off, and he didn't have any idea what he'd said to do it.

"Sounds reasonable to me." He defended.

"Well it doesn't to me. Everyone would be feeling sorry for me, pitying me. No—no way. You forget, I have to live here after you are gone. I won't have it."

"Okay, then maybe it'll be the other way around." He smiled at her.

She glared at him. "What other way around?"

"You'll throw me out, for—good, old, Burt."

"For good old Burt?" Her expression grew puzzled, and then she frowned at him again.

"Well, I assumed you were sorta—sweet on the fella." He began, not knowing where this would take him and wishing he hadn't started this particular conversation.

"I'm not sweet on anyone! Good grief Burt's old enough to be my father..." She practically barked at him.

He smiled to himself, at least she saw that much. "And that won't work either. Everyone would hate me and think me an adulteress. I won't have it! I just won't have it. It's easy for you. You won't have to live here afterwards." Her lips thinned with anger.

"Well, you got any better ideas?" His curt tone lashed at her.

Hannah was silent again for a moment. Then as tough it finally occurred to her, she nodded. "We just say it didn't work out. We got two ranches, you wanted to go home, I didn't want to go with you, and leave them to draw their own conclusions. We could call it a separation at first, then as time goes on a divorce."

The word divorce hung in Rusty's crawl. He didn't like the sound of that cold, and unfeeling word.

"Okay...sounds reasonable." He amended not wanting to rile her any further. It was getting them nowhere to fight over something that would mean absolutely nothing to her anyway.

She stared at him hard and long, and then something gave within her. As though she had made her mind up to co-operate to some degree.

"Okay, I'll go along with the wedding, against my better judgment. I'll even go along with the preacher. But that's all the bending I'm gonna do." She flushed miserably, as though it pained her to give in.

"Fair enough," Rusty said letting out a long audible breath then he stood up from the table. He liked the fact that she had sense enough to know when to stop fighting. "Now, let's get these dishes washed."

She looked at him queerly. "You wash dishes?"

"Yes ma'am. I was taught to clean up after myself."

He answered with a smile and a wink.

*****

Hannah scrubbed each dish a long time. She needed this time to sort out what she'd agreed to.

Why had she let him woo her into a wedding? Probably because he had used a cool impersonal tone in his voice. Detachment. But still, a wedding meant dressing up and acting as though she cared about this cowboy. No one that knew her would believe it for a minute. Would they? Of course, she hadn't been around many of her neighbors for a while, since she hadn't lived here in a while. They really didn't know her as well as she made him believe.

Her courage and determination to keep this ranch had brought her to this!

She glanced at him out of the corner of her eye and fretted. He was too handsome, too sure of himself. Normally she wouldn't like this kind of man. But he did have a few redeeming qualities that she couldn't dismiss. He demanded respect, he was a gentleman, and he seemed to share her love of animals, and he was a helluva cowboy. She couldn't fault him for any of these things. Still, she couldn't weaken around him either. He'd hurt her, break her heart and she knew it.

She had to keep herself in check at all times around Rusty Travers, he was simply too dangerous to her heart. She'd already set the rules, she had to abide by them.

When the dishes were done, they went to check on the dog. He seemed to be resting comfortably. He whined when Hannah scratched behind his ears and licked her hands. Despite her hard reserve, her heart seemed to turn to mush around this little mutt.

Walking back to the ranch house Rusty put his arm around her and they chatted in a very friendly way. If he'd been the least bit flirty, she probably would have moved away, but he kept it casual and friendly.

"What should we call him?" Rusty asked.

"Who?"

"The dog."

"Oh...I don't know. You pick a name, it's your dog."

"Okay, how about Jugs."

"Jugs?" She looked at him with a slight frown.

"You don't like it?"

"I was thinking about Pepper. You know, he's got those black spots all over him."

"Pepper...okay, Pepper it is."

That settled, it seemed they might be getting along until he mentioned the date.

"Date?"

"Look darlin'," he stopped, stared down into her frowning face and smiled. "We have to figure out when we're going to tie the knot. It'll be one of those whirlwind courtships. Just let me handle this part of it, okay. We'll have dinner in town a couple of times, so people see us together. Might even take in a Sunday service or two. And I'd say the sooner the better, wouldn't you?"

No, she wouldn't. She wasn't sure she made the right decision and she wanted to back out. How had he gotten control of the whole event? But she knew she was in trouble. Especially when he smiled at her. It did strange things to her insides. Things she didn't want to deal with or acknowledge.

"My name is Hannah," she said huskily.

"I know." He answered just as huskily as they stood on the porch facing one another. All kidding aside, the air thickened with a new tension. How had they turned a perfectly normal conversation into this new friction between them. The air sizzled. Crackled even!

"Not Darlin'." she said almost breathlessly, forcing herself to think about anything but being close to this man. It was impossible. Why did the air seem so full of him?

His glance slid to her mouth.

Her palms began to sweat. It wasn't going to happen. It couldn't...but—

"Humor me, engaged couples often call each other pet names. I wouldn't be offended if you called me something sweet." His mouth twitched.

"I'd like to call you something, but it wouldn't be sweet," she murmured.

"Now Darlin', we can't fight all the time." He was inches from her now.

Damn him for smiling. Didn't he know he was a charmer when he smiled? She didn't want to be charmed. Especially by a cowboy that was going to be leaving soon.

"It kinda fits," he said coming closer and bending slightly to see into her face.

Their eyes met and locked. His glance was gentle and contemplative. Her world seemed to rock on its heels. As though someone had punched her in the stomach and told her not to breathe.

"I'm not your Darlin'. Your anything. Do you understand?" Why did her voice falter, and almost hitch when she looked into those all-seeing blue eyes?

She was nearly nose to nose with him now. Too close, her heart warned. The air seemed to expel between them.

Heat radiated like a brilliant sun shining between them. Yet the moonlight twinkled in his gaze.

It was in that briefest of moments, when he sighed with such exasperation just before he brought her closer and kissed her softly on the mouth. As though he really didn't plan on doing it, thought better of it, but couldn't quite prevent it.

She gasped as he pulled away and her intentional dismay turned to mush when he covered her mouth fully with his own. Again!

And to her own embarrassment, she wrapped her arms around his neck and hung on for the ride.

She was astounded at his mastery of the kiss. She was drowning, she was sure of it. Being pulled purposely under by some force greater than her own will. Never had her senses been shattered by a mere kiss.

Playing with fire, that's what she was doing. Not water, fire, she repeated in her head. Tiny sparks of wildfire shot through her as he deepened the kiss and she mindlessly pulled him closer and added her own fuel to the fire. Her mind ordered her to struggle, but he made her forget that order. He made her squash it in the back of her mind, stow it for later. He made her swoon instead. He made her come alive, like a lifeless puppet suddenly brought to awe-stirring life. He awakened the hunger for love she had long ago stifled. And made her want more, so much more.

She'd been kissed before, her mind swam in a hopeless, mindless swirl—but never so thoroughly. Never as though her lips belonged to his. It seemed oddly as though when he touched her, she had been branded. A Travers brand. She had no will, no good sense...

A coyote howled in the distance and he slowly pulled away. His eyes sparkled in the moonlight. "Yeah," his voice was like a whisper. "I think Darlin' fits just fine."

She was sure she was red to the toes, but thankfully he couldn't see that. To think she had returned his kiss so blatantly!

She needed to say something, anything, but her voice escaped her for the moment.

He smiled. "Night, Darlin'."

*****

So, the little ice maiden wasn't so icy after all? That kiss had floored him. He wasn't prepared to deal with its effects. Not just yet anyway. And certainly not with her!

What was wrong with him? He'd been in love with Jennifer so long, and now in a matter of days he was being pulled into some sort of magnetism he couldn't understand, with a woman he certainly couldn't read.

But for some reason he felt merry and light hearted and wanted to run and shout. Instead he whistled an old Spanish tune he'd heard in the bunkhouse a time or two. His heart suddenly knew something his head wasn't reading.

He had to admit, she puzzled him. She looked like a little clown in those baggy clothes. She acted like a horse's ass most of the time. But the woman could definitely kiss!

And better than Jennifer too!

# Chapter Five

The first date went reasonably easy; Hannah reflected as she combed her hair and then crammed the hat on her head. Dear God, who would have ever thought she'd be dating a man these days. But then, it wasn't for real, so maybe it didn't count, she reasoned. Rusty had taken her into Pecos, the nearest town, to the best little restaurant and ordered steaks. The waitress was surprised to see her and seemed anxious to get to know Rusty too. Curiosity always lurked in small towns. But Hannah hadn't given it that much thought. Even though she'd graduated here in Pecos, she hadn't been a regular visitor to town in years.

She'd donned a pair of new Levi's, and a pink sweater that was anything but revealing. She wore her hair down and without the hat, and Rusty seemed surprised and pleased.

She hadn't worn tight jeans like most women her age. Her wardrobe was overly modest, and she preferred to keep it that way. She knew from working Vegas that the more a girl advertised the more the men took the bait, and she didn't want any more kisses from Rusty. At least that's what she told herself a dozen times a day. So why was her brain fastened on that kiss on the porch. Why couldn't she get it off her mind? And exactly how would she manage to avoid them since he seemed determined to convince the entire population of Texas that they were in love.

During dinner he'd talked about his place. From the way he spoke of his family, she knew he was close to them and it hit home hard. She wanted to be close to her brother Jimmy too, but it was miles that separated them, and his life was a busy one too, now that he had a practice.

Rusty was more than eager to meet her friends and introduce himself as her "man". The thought seemed silly.

Her "man". She could just hear her friends now, "Hannah has a man."

She didn't need a man. Since Vic Trusdale had been caught in her girlfriend's bed, she had quickly decided that men were a commodity she could do without. How she had ever let herself in for such a fall she didn't know. But she vowed to never let it happen again. No man would make an idiot out of her again.

She hadn't analyzed how she felt about Vic lately, but at the time she was sure she had loved him. A sucker, that's what she had been. Well, no more.

She had to admit though, when Rusty brought her home, with no goodnight kiss, she was disappointed. After all, kissing Rusty was a totally new experience and she needed to know more about him, about what made him tick. At least that's what she told herself. That's how she explained it to herself as she tried desperately not to show her disappointment.

*****

She was in the middle of going to town for some much-needed supplies the next day when Pepper ran out to greet her. The dog happily wagged his tail and nudged his head at her legs until she reached down to pet him. Seeing his instant affection, she laughed and played with him for a few minutes.

She couldn't stop the giggle bursting forth when he jumped on her leg and licked at her hands and face.

"You really are just a big pet, aren't you?" She laughed and took his head into her hands and scratched behind his ears. He whined and licked her cheek. She laughed, delighted with the dog's affectionate greeting.

Then Burt rode up. "Never thought I'd see the day when you'd be sportin' a pet."

Hannah whipped about, and Pepper ran off, barking at Burt's obvious interruption. "He's not my pet."

"Shore does act like he is." Burt spit his tobacco in the opposite direction.

"He belongs to Mr. Travers," she said in a clipped voice. Annoyed that Burt was so hostile about everything that concerned Rusty, she tried to change the subject, but Burt wouldn't let her.

"Kissin' a man usually entitles you to a first name, now don't it." Burt said low and with a hint of anger.

Hannah glanced up at him and saw the reprimand in his eyes. It shocked her. Burt had no right making remarks like that.

So, he'd seen them the other night on the porch. Or had he been watching them? A slow creeping feeling ran up her spine as she tossed him a quick frown. The fact that he'd actually spied on her made her angry.

"You're right, it's Rusty's dog."

She reached up to pet his horse on his forehead. "Want me to go with you into town?" Burt asked eyeing her keenly.

"No," she answered curtly. Then realizing she was short with him, she softened her voice, "I'm not getting that much." Hannah was accustomed to inviting Burt to go into town with her, but she didn't like his tone of voice and quickly decided against it. She didn't like him spying on her either. In fact, Burt was annoying her no end since Rusty came here and she'd had about all she could take. She realized she would have to deal with Burt somehow, but she didn't know exactly how to handle the situation yet.

Naturally, she couldn't fire Burt. Especially over something like this, but she would have to put Burt in his place soon, if he didn't stop getting into her business.

Burt frowned down at her, not bothering to hide his feelings. "I saw you goin' out with him last night. How'd it go?"

"Fine, Burt. Now I better go so I can get back before dark. Did you move the herd to the south pasture?"

Burt studied her face a moment, and then with a brooding frown he nodded. "Sure, I did."

"Good, see you later, then."

"You don't have to do this, you know?" He offered, coming closer so the horse nuzzled her cheek.

She glanced up at him and squinted in the noon day sun. "Yes, I do, Burt. Yes, I do."

He tipped his hat and left, as though someone had put a burr under his saddle. It was easy to see Burt wasn't happy with her decision, but it was her decision. He'd have to learn to live with it. She was.

Rusty had seen the exchange from the corral but he said nothing, a good thing. She didn't want to talk about Burt. He was becoming harder to handle and she just didn't want to talk about their relationship or lack of one with anyone right now. Rusty Travers had agreed to help her save this ranch, and despite her personal opinion of him, which she was no longer sure about, she appreciated his open honesty. She wanted to get this ranch paid for and have Rusty Travers go home, so things could get back to normal. Whatever normal had been.

But then normal didn't appeal to her either. Not now. Rusty Travers had somehow changed that too. She couldn't remember what a normal day was like anymore. She'd never worked alongside a man like Rusty before, a man as used to giving orders as taking.

When she returned from town, Rusty was fixing supper in her kitchen. Josey wasn't in sight and Hannah couldn't stop herself from gaping.

"I didn't know you cooked too," she laughed as she brought two bags of groceries inside and placed them on the counter.

"Yes ma'am. And wait until you taste my chili." He smiled with amusement. He glanced at her bags and then her. His glance slid over her with silent appreciation. "Anymore outside?"

"No, this is it." Her cheeks colored from his quick assessment.

She put the groceries up then leaned against the counter and watched him. He seemed to know what he was doing, and it was refreshing to have a man wait on her. A very new experience.

But when he brought a sample of his culinary arts to her mouth with a wooden spoon, she went white then red. It seemed so intimate the way he touched her lips with the spoon. She was filled with an excitement she couldn't explain. Boy was her imagination wandering these days. It wasn't like the Roman Gods feeding each other grapes, for heaven's sake. This was a ranch, and the food was chili. She had to quit attaching romance to such trivial things and Rusty Travers.

"Come on now. You gotta taste it and tell me if I left anything out." He encouraged dabbing her bottom lip with the spoon.

Hannah didn't taste a thing but took it into her mouth and swallowed.

Then her eyes watered, and she gasped. "Water." She choked.

Rusty quickly filled a glass and handed it to her. "Too hot, huh?"

"A little," she choked again, this time coughing hard.

He patted her on the back and she pinked again. His mere touch sent quivers of delight up her spine. She tried to act unaffected but knew she hadn't succeeded by the devilish look in his eyes.

Thinking she was still on fire, he took her in his arms and consoled her a bit, "Hey Darlin' I didn't mean to knock your socks off."

She heard the rapid thump of his heart, smelled the intoxicating odor of a man who'd worked up a sweat, and felt an immediate heat growing between them. She wanted to pull away, but she looked up at him and then it happened again. He kissed her!

Damn! The chili was forgotten. All that seemed important at the moment was this warm, inviting kiss that went on forever. This time was no different, her hands stole up and around his neck to pull him closer as she sighed into his arms. As though she needed this kiss to steady her.

That was silly, of course she didn't need his kisses, her mind corrected, but his soft massaging lips sent her sense of reason way beyond the kitchen. He conjured up pictures of ecstasy in her mind that were nowhere near a kitchen.

Their bodies seemed to melt into each other, as his arms went around her waist. She had the greatest urge to curl a leg around his, but at the moment, she couldn't move, she was sure she was nothing more than a pool of hot butter. After all, she hadn't been thinking at all, just reacting.

His tongue gently flicked against her lips and he tasted the remnants of chili on her mouth. He licked his lips, slowly. Her eyes followed his actions and he kissed her again, this time she opened her mouth to his. The kiss went on forever, their tongues exploring shyly at first, then urgently, until both of them were breathless and panting when they pulled away.

Hannah turned away just as Burt came through the kitchen door. She needed time to assimilate what was happening to her. Time to catch her breath and come down to earth, if the earth was still there.

Burt didn't hide his displeasure, he seemed to recognize he'd interrupted, but he didn't apologize. Instead, he frowned at her and went back out, slamming the door.

"I guess ole Burt didn't like what he saw." Rusty chuckled.

Hannah grew red and angry. She was furious at her own vulnerability to this man. Mad at herself more than him. "Next time we better have a bigger audience than Burt when you do that."

Next time, was she completely insane? There shouldn't be a next time. Ever! A few more kisses like that and she be hauling him into the bedroom herself. No sir, she didn't need or want his kisses. Or did she?

"Yes, ma'am." Rusty's relaxed smile told her he was much more composed after that kiss than she, and she could be in big trouble if she let it get out of hand.

They ate the chili in guarded silence. Perhaps he had some reservations as to how far he carried the kiss. He certainly should. And she had reservations about her own actions.

In truth Hannah couldn't lay all the blame on Rusty for that kiss. She'd wanted it as much as he did. She could have pulled free and slapped his face. But for some reason, beyond her own knowledge, she wanted him to kiss her again. She just wished Rusty wasn't so darn good at it! She kept thinking each time would prove it was just an over active imagination on her part. She had to prove to herself that his kisses weren't any different than anyone else's.

She'd sworn off men after leaving Vegas. After being dumped by the man she called her boyfriend, Vic Trusdale, she had given up on ever meeting Mr. Right. Instead, she wanted to go home, and never worry about a man again. Only that hadn't happened either. Even as dismally as she dressed, Burt had pursued her. She wasn't sure why. Perhaps he felt protective of her, since he'd known her since a child. But the look in his eyes today wasn't protective. She couldn't understand Burt, but she knew she wasn't interested in a man his age. She'd always thought of him as sort of an Uncle. What astonished her was that Burt didn't seem to see it.

*****

It was a bitter cold Wednesday and Hannah had been working on the old windmill for most of the morning when a Ford station-wagon pulled up into the yard. In it were three girls that Hannah had gone to school with, girls that seldom came to visit, unless they had a mighty good reason.

Still, Hannah was glad to see them.

Dusting her clothes off, Hannah made her way off the porch toward the car. It was times like this she wished she did wear nicer clothes. She felt like a real rag doll beside them.

"Samantha, Sandy, and Cora Mae, what in the world are you three doing out here?" Hannah asked as though she had no idea. Of course, she did know why they came. They wanted to get a first-hand look at her so called "boyfriend".

Samantha got out of the car first and ran toward her. She hugged Hannah and smiled, "It's been so long, Hannah."

Hannah blushed and nodded shyly. "I guess it has."

Samantha had once been a little chubby, but now she looked gorgeous in her tan suede pantsuit. Hannah had always liked Samantha, she was quiet most of the time and not as nosey as the other two. Samantha's hair was different now, cut a little shorter, it was golden brown and hung just to her shoulders. It flattered her face. Her green eyes sparkled with mischief.

"Too long for old friends like us, Hannah."

"Old friends, I've been home quite a while and you've not bothered, why now?" Damn, that was downright catty, but she couldn't stop her words in time. She honestly liked Samantha, but the other two had things on their minds from the looks on their faces.

She silently wished she had the time to chit-chat with the girls and catch up on all the goings on. But she knew better. Ranch life left little time for such idle things.

"We heard you were pretty near engaged. And you haven't so much as bothered to tell a soul about it. What gives girl?" Sandy said as she got out of the car and came up to the porch. She didn't hug Hannah and Hannah was grateful. Sandy and Cora Mae didn't come to see her, she knew. She eyed Sandy closely.

Sandy was tall and thin and carried an almost elegant air about her. Her dark hair swayed against her shoulders.

Hannah hesitated a moment, remembering that Cora Mae was the banker's niece. Of course, she would know about Rusty being here. Perhaps her Uncle had sent her out here to find out what was going on, firsthand.

She glanced at Cora Mae getting out of the car and gasped at her outrageously tight outfit. Cora Mae had literally been stuffed into those jeans and the blouse she wore displayed her perfect eight figure. Cora Mae personified the word 'dumb blonde'.

Hannah couldn't stop the slight blush and floundered on how to handle this one. She knew the town's people would get curious, but she forgot about some of her old school friends. She'd like to think she still had friends when this was all over as she confessed her engagement.

"His name's Rusty Travers, and yes, we're sorta unofficially engaged." Hannah tried to sound normal, but it was hard to be normal when lies were coming out of her mouth as fast as flies on a watermelon.

Maybe she should just go back to Vegas and all this wouldn't be happening to her. But no, she'd never go back there. She hadn't fit in then, and she wouldn't fit in now.

"The Rusty Travers, from the 4 Bar None?"

"That's right," Hannah confirmed Cora's outburst.

She saw the dollar signs in Cora Mae's ultra-blue eyes."... And yes, it's true. But I didn't know their ranch was that famous."

Cora Mae glanced at her strangely as she stepped up on the porch. She didn't hug Hannah either.

Cora Mae's makeup resembled the kind Hannah had to wear in Vegas and she nearly laughed at the effigy.

"Why, everyone knows about the Travers bunch. Best ranchers, richest bachelors, and downright gorgeous men in Texas. And have the State Champion Breeders to boot."

Word had certainly gotten around as to who Rusty was.

"Oh, the ranch isn't what everyone knows them for, though, hon," Cora Mae emphasized."...the brothers are the best looking bunch of cowboys this side of the Rio."

Samantha's disapproving brow went up a notch, but she didn't say anything.

Cora Mae saw Samantha's reaction and added, "Well they are, honey. And don't be too condescending, you had a bigger than Texas crush on Jake some time back as I recall. For all the good it did you. That Jake wouldn't give any woman the time of day, he's just too serious."

Samantha blushed this time and looked away from everyone's probing glance.

Cora Mae smiled and turned her attention back to Hannah.

"How'd you meet him? I'm sure I've never heard you speak of him before?"

Cora Mae leaned against the porch railing in a model-like pose, looking very much like Marilyn Monroe, and sounding like a lawyer well into an interrogation.

Hannah stood there staring at them and trying desperately to figure out what her answer would be. "Come on in the house and we'll have some hot chocolate, it's too cold to stand out here and talk." At least she remembered her manners.

An hour later Hannah found herself knee deep in lies and butterflies. It had been a long time since she'd spent this much time talking to old friends, and it felt good, except for the lies. It would have been more fun if the girls had actually come to see her, but she knew they wanted to get a glance at Rusty.

Then Rusty himself walked in, dusting his boots off at the door, and seeing she had company, politely kissed her on the cheek and took his hat off.

"Ladies..."

"Are you The Rusty Travers?" they all choired.

"Yes ma'am."

Hannah was still in shock, but she quickly recovered from the kiss and introduced them. Rusty ignored her embarrassment asked for a cup of hot chocolate, too.

Jealousy? No, she wasn't jealous of them? Was she? Where had that come from? You had to really like someone to be jealous, didn't you?

She wanted to throw the hot chocolate at him the way he was eyeing Cora Mae and that tight-fitting blouse. He was a red-necked cowboy and he deserved to be embarrassed. Still, she was supposed to be engaged to him, and for every angry moment, she realized it would be worse to embarrass herself and him with her pet peeve. These three girls were the nosiest busybodies in Pecos and most everyone knew it. All except for Samantha, and she had a hunch Samantha might be after some news of Jake Travers.

He probably didn't know that Cora Mae was out here spying on them for her Uncle either.

"I'm glad to meet you ladies. Hannah is such a busy little rancher she seldom has company. But I've wanted to meet some of her friends for a while now." Rusty was saying as she returned with his drink.

"Thanks, Darlin'." He winked at her as his gaze rested on her still moist lips.

The desire in his eyes surprised her, shocked her, and pleased her.

"It's so unlike Hannah to be dating anyone, we absolutely had to come and see for ourselves. I for one, didn't believe it. Why, she hasn't so much as bothered with dating since she's been home." Cora Mae said adjusting her shirt so Rusty could get a better view of her fine figure. Subtle, she wasn't.

But it was Sandy who stepped up to him and smiled. Sandy wasn't usually a flirt, but her actions intrigued Hannah. "Rusty Travers, aren't you Deke Travers' brother?"

"Yes ma'am, you know my brother?"

"We attended a couple of auctions with him a few years back, didn't we Samantha? And Clint too. He's been riding the bulls for years at the rodeo in Pecos."

Samantha nodded, but continued to eye Rusty suspiciously as though she didn't believe a word Hannah had told them. If anyone had any brains in this group Samantha did, and Hannah knew she had better play her part or the whole thing would blow up in their faces, and after all the lies she just told she couldn't face them with the truth.

"Deke's married now." Rusty exclaimed obviously intrigued by Sandy's open curiosity.

"Married? No one ever thought he'd get married. He was always so shy around women."

"He got out of that when he met Emma." Rusty smiled and put his arm around Hannah as though to let her know he knew these women were simply being nosy and he wanted to ham it up as much as possible. The man was impossible, but adorable.

"What about Jake and Clint?" Samantha suddenly asked.

"Jake's over in Peaceful, he's the Sheriff now. He's always wanted to be a lawman, although I'll confess, we thought he was going to be a lawyer. Clint and Abby got married."

"They finally tied the knot? Lord that girl was crazy in love with Clint most of his life and he never had a clue." Cora Mae said, casting Rusty a slightly flirtatious glance.

"Clint sure could have had any number of girls when he rode the circuit."

"Yeah." Rusty glanced about for a second and smiled at them, "And I didn't realize they were so well known, either." Rusty winked.

"Oh, don't pay any attention to us. Word gets around in little towns. Anyone who is anyone is practically in the newspapers. Besides our Samantha here, had a crush on Jake for years, but never let on." Cora Mae blurted out. "Everyone that goes to the rodeos knows Clint or has heard of him. Boy he could ride. We heard he quit the circuit, is it true?"

"Yes, ma'am. Took a good woman to put a stop to that." Rusty grinned at her.

"Jake was such a quiet man. You say he moved to Peaceful?" Samantha seemed to file this information for later use. Hannah had heard Samantha speak of Jake Travers several times and knew she still carried a torch for the cowboy. Obviously, Jake Travers had no clue, or wasn't interested.

"Yes, he's been there quite a while."

"Well, I'm sure he wouldn't remember me, I was quite pudgy back then. Round as a barrel."

"Maybe you should have told him you liked him. He's a little on the shy side too. Especially around women." Rusty's infectious grin set the mood in the room. "You'd be surprised what a man remembers about a woman. A voice, eye contact, even an attitude."

"Jake was always so serious..." Samantha's voice drifted off as though she were thinking of Jake.

"That's Jake alright."

"And you and Hannah—are you really engaged?" Cora Mae asked as though she had every right to.

Rusty's mouth twitched, his eyes gleamed and then he got up, went into the back bedroom and came out again, mysteriously silent, but carrying a small black box with him. Hannah bristled. What was he up to now? She could handle these girls alone. She didn't need him prodding them on.

"I'm hoping this makes it official," he grinned at the other ladies and dropped down on one knee, his all but somber face staring at Hannah.

Dear God, at the dramatics he was willing to go through, Hannah grimaced.

The girls gasped, as though they knew exactly what he was up to.

His eyes landed on Hannah with nothing short of animal lust. How could he turn on the heat in his eyes so quickly? "I was gonna wait until tonight, Darlin' but I don't see why I have to now. This being Valentine's day, it's only fitting I ask you today. Will you marry me, Hannah?"

Hannah stood staring at the small black box he presented to her. She heard the other girls gasp again, and softly laughed. She knew it was a ring, but she was speechless. First because he offered it, and second because he made such a spectacle of doing so. Down on his knees, for heaven sake, she wanted to throttle him. She'd give him a piece of her mind later.

"Well say something, girl," Cora Mae urged her. "I'd certainly be saying something if someone gave me a proposal like that!"

Hannah felt a lump in her throat and tried to speak, but her voice didn't sound like her own.

"Rusty, this is so," She glanced down into his face, but there wasn't a sign of mockery there. "—unexpected. I mean...I thought we were gonna wait a while."

"No use waiting when I know exactly what I want. Will you marry me, Darlin'?"

His smile was beguiling, his manners impeccable. Hannah took the box from his hand and opened it. She expected a modest little five and dime ring that would be easily forgotten but choked when she saw the two-carat diamond staring back at her.

She heard the other girls gasp again! Talk about impressions.

Good grief what was he doing? Why was he being so dramatic? He could easily have bought a cheap ring and put it on her finger. But this—she hadn't expected. Of course, it had to be big, she thought in retrospect, he was impressing these people with his money. And word of this hunk of rock would certainly get around town fast enough.

Tears welled in her eyes though, and the genuine feeling of being totally overwhelmed hit her. She tried to say something, anything, but, how could she? The diamond was huge, and the most beautiful thing she'd ever seen.

Rusty stood up, smiled and took the ring and slid it on her finger, "I love you Hannah. Just say yes," he whispered throatily.

If he'd have been an actor, he couldn't have played the part any better.

"Y-yes," she finally managed, as a tear slipped down her cheek and she quickly swatted it away as the girls' laughter embarrassed her.

Without hesitation Rusty stole her from their clutches and hauled her into his arms and kissed her as though he meant every word of it.

Lost in the kiss, Hannah tasted her tears, and the exquisite taste of Rusty Travers. She was quickly growing fond of those kisses and wondered how she was going to ever give them up.

With that sobering thought, she gently pushed him away, and gasped. "You overwhelmed me."

That kiss left no doubt as to his intentions and the women crowded around her to admire the beautiful stone and wish her all the best. There was no need to worry now, all three of them believed he meant business.

The girls stayed to dinner and Rusty wasn't caught two steps away from Hannah all evening. Did he honestly think she would screw it all up or something?

Hannah felt baffled at her own inability to cope, and the embarrassment at how they made over her new engagement. Even Cora Mae bought the entire act, hook, line and sinker.

But something niggled in the back of Hannah's mind. Most men didn't run around with a ring in their pocket. So where did this one suddenly materialize from? And he certainly hadn't expected these ladies to show up on her doorstep.

Could this have been for the girl he really loved, somewhere? That thought put a damper on her excitement, but she played out the part until everyone left. She glanced down at the ring, and the lump in her throat felt suddenly bigger, more painful.

Late that evening Rusty was sitting on the porch, drinking in the twinkling of stars when she joined him. She had to admit, she'd never met a man who enjoyed all the simple pleasures that he did. Pepper, a ride at dawn, and star gazing.

"Where's the ring?" he demanded when she sat beside him on the swing.

She didn't look at him. "It's on the window sill in the kitchen. I didn't think I should wear something that big doing the dishes."

He nodded. "That sounds reasonable. Just don't forget to put it back on."

"So, who does it belong to?" She asked still not looking directly at him.

"You, of course," he added with a decided frown when she finally looked up at him.

"No, I mean, who did it belong to?" She asked softly.

"No one," he said quietly looking away.

"Look, you don't have to talk about it if you don't want to, but men don't go around with chunks of diamonds that big every day." She explained. "A man doesn't buy that kind of ring for a girl he hasn't even met yet. It belongs to someone, doesn't it?"

He shrugged. "No, I never got around to asking her, but that doesn't matter. Now word will get around, and it will be no secret that I've got money for this ranch. That's good. Besides, it doesn't matter."

Something in his voice, told her it did matter and for a second, she put her own feelings aside and really looked at him this time. Whoever the girl was, he had loved her, and she wouldn't make light of the situation.

"Who was she?"

"She? She who?" He asked getting up and standing by the porch railing as though suddenly cornered and not liking it.

"The girl that made you buy that ring."

For a moment he looked as though he wasn't going to say anything, and then he hung his head and in a low husky voice he answered.

"I guess you gotta right to know. Her name was Jennifer. We grew up together." He paused glancing at Hannah to see her reaction. "I loved her all my life, almost. Thought she felt the same. Then one day she just up and leaves, without a word. I haven't heard from her since."

Hannah watched his face contort into a million different shades of hurt and wanted to go and comfort him but knew that was unwise. Instead she stayed where she was. But her voice carried sympathy and respect.

"I'm sorry. You must have loved her dearly." Hannah heard herself say.

"Yeah, well, little good that did. She didn't care."

"Maybe and then maybe she didn't know what she wanted."

"Maybe," he glanced at her then.

"It's a beautiful ring, Rusty."

He nodded. "I'm glad you like it."

"I'll take very good care of it for you." Hannah said trying to console him.

"Yeah, I think you will."

"What was she like?" She had to ask, had to know.

"Jennifer?"

She nodded.

"She was blonde, gorgeous. Had a figure that wouldn't quit. She had so much vitality. Wanted to do everything."

"Everything, huh?" Hannah glanced away, then back at him.

"Maybe that's why she left."

"What do you mean?"

"I mean, when someone grows up in one place all their life, they can sometimes feel stifled. They want to experience more."

Rusty stared at her now openly assessing her. "Yeah, I just never looked at it that way."

"Maybe you should. Maybe it wasn't you she left. Maybe it was her yearning to learn and explore the world, that she wanted so badly."

Rusty studied her a long minute before replying. "You talk like you know the feeling."

She smothered a soft laugh. "I did...once."

"Oh, so you explored it and got bored and came home then?"

She didn't want to talk about herself. Didn't want to bring herself into the conversation.

"You might say that."

"What kind of work did you do, Hannah?"

The question didn't startle her so much as the way he ask it. As though he meant to uncover a secret about her past. It was only fair that she share something of herself too, but that was one thing she wouldn't be sharing with anyone. At least not unless she had to.

"It was a good job and paid extraordinary money."

"I gathered that. So why didn't you stay at it?"

"I guess I was never cut out for city work." She said and got up and started for the door. He might be curious, but he wasn't going to be hanging around, and there was no use telling him everything. He probably wouldn't be interested anyway.

"Running away, Hannah. What deep dark secret are you carrying around?"

"I'm not." She turned and looked at him again. A mistake, because his eyes seemed to capture hers.

"Look, we're gonna get married, it certainly wouldn't hurt to know a little more about each other. If we don't talk this out, how can we begin to answer questions that others might ask?"

"What questions? What others?"

"The kind people start asking when you get married and join other groups and stuff."

"Who said anything about joining anyone? We owe no one any explanations." Her voice rose with frustration.

"Just each other."

She turned to look at him squarely, a mistake again because the look on his face was seriously causing her pulse to rise. Everything about Rusty Travers made her come alive and she didn't like it one bit. She'd made up her mind a long time ago not to let anyone into her heart again. And she meant to keep that promise to herself. The one thing Hannah O'Leary wouldn't do again, is be a fool.

But conversation couldn't cause a problem and she was open to talking. It might even help to get a few things off her chest. Anything except talking about her job. She wasn't ready to confess everything...just yet.

She sat down, sighing as though it took a lot of restraint not to object to his inquiry.

"You want to know about me?" She asked bluntly.

"Sure. Aren't you even a little curious about me?"

"Maybe—just a little."

"So—"

"Look, there's nothing to tell. I've lived mostly a very sedate life here on the ranch. I grew up here. My mother is buried out there, under that big oak. Dad made a small cemetery there. He promised that no matter what we'd never sell this land—not as long as she is buried there. That's part of the reason this land means so much to me. I can't leave her." Her voice came to a squeak and she realized tears were close to falling.

"When did she die?"

"Years ago. When I was little. I remember how she loved to sing and read to me. I remember being in the kitchen with her. She'd put me up on the counter and talk and sing to me while she fixed supper for Dad. I remember—so many little things about her, and yet, sometimes—sometimes they all seem like I dreamed them up. You know?"

"Yeah, I think I do." He cleared his throat. "My Mama died when I was born, as I'm sure you already know. I've felt responsible for that all my life. As though I killed her. I've watched my dad mourn her death for years. And yet, I have no recollection of her at all. Just a picture, that's all."

"That's worse, no memories...." Hannah choked on her words. "But Rusty, you can't hold yourself responsible for her death."

It was as though some common bond had grown between them, as though they reached out and touched one another in that instant. The same heart-breaking feeling of loss. Hannah took a deep breath. Don't let him get to you. He isn't staying!

"That's why this land is so important to me."

"Yeah," came his throaty reply as he looked down at her. "I think I understand that part of you Hannah."

A warmth stole over her as she looked up at him and he smiled at her. It was like the very first time he really saw her for what she was, and it startled her. No one had come that close to her before and it scared her!

Afraid she had let too much of herself out, she stood again and started for the door.

A hand reached out and took hers, softly, not pulling, just holding.

"I promise you Hannah, you'll keep this land." Rusty said and squeezed her hand until she looked at him again.

A tear spilled, and she looked away. "Thank you," she whispered and went inside.

## *Chapter Six*

Rusty wrestled with his feelings that night. He didn't want to marry Hannah. And not just because she wasn't as pretty as Jennifer, either. If the truth were known, he'd have to admit, he was beginning to like Hannah—a lot. Not because she was alluring exactly, although there was something about her that attracted him, he just couldn't put his finger on it. Hannah wasn't like most the women he had known.

No, but because marrying her would be a big lie. And she didn't deserve that. Not Hannah, she was honest, hardworking, a good person. He liked her. Still, the sooner he did marry her and get the loan approved, the sooner he could go back to his own place, his own life.

His own place. That was the problem. It had never really been his place and he knew it. And until recently he hadn't thought much about the fact that it was Deke's place, and Dad's home. But it wasn't his. Not since he'd grown up. He didn't run things, Deke did. Through the years he had felt more like a ranch hand than part owner, even though Deke did everything to make him part of the 4 Bar None.

He reasoned that since he'd been here, he'd helped run this ranch as much as he had at home. Maybe more. The boys in the bunkhouse had grown to like and respect him. They knew he knew his business. He liked it here. The boys had gradually come to accept him, all but Burt. Burt didn't like him, but at least he was honest about it. And he knew it had nothing to do with the ranch or the way he gave him orders.

Why Hannah didn't see through that wrangler he couldn't begin to understand. He was simply too old for her. Hannah wasn't ugly, she wouldn't win any prizes, especially the way she dressed, but there was something very appealing about the little lady. Something deeper than looks.

It wasn't his business, and yet it was. He was the one fixing to marry her.

Rusty thought about Deke and Emma, how happy they were. Marriage had always seemed like a likely solution when he was with Jennifer. But now there was Hannah and it was a big lie and somehow, he felt like as big a heel as Burt.

He tried to conjure up Jennifer now like he had always done before, but for some reason he was having trouble with that. He couldn't quite remember how her eyes looked. How could he forget what she looked like? He'd dated her for years. Been with her practically every day. Then she up and went away, without a word. Women...he didn't need them.

He heard Hannah's bed creak and he knew she was lying down, most likely just opposite him on the other side of the wall. He wondered if she went straight to sleep or laid there thinking half the night like him.

He wondered if she wore pretty little gowns or flannel or maybe nothing at all. Whoa...He didn't need to be thinking along those lines. He'd never be in her bed, and he shouldn't even go there, but the sound of those springs kept him ever alert and constantly wondering about Hannah.

He might be getting married, but he doubted seriously if Hannah would ever welcome him in her bed. His thoughts had no right being there. But sometimes a man couldn't control thoughts. And as long as it was just thoughts it was harmless.

The next day Rusty was riding fence, wondering when the cold spell would break, and hints of spring might appear. He missed the wildflowers that dotted the pastures in the early spring. He enjoyed the spring calving and branding time. Not the monotonous winter when there was little else to do but chip blocks of ice for water, mend fences and make repairs for spring. Besides, it had been an exceptionally cold winter, and spring would change all that

Hannah came riding up to him in a hurry, breaking his thoughts, and handed him her cell phone. "You've got a call."

Rusty glanced at her in surprise. He didn't even know she had a cell phone. It never rang. She was wearing her usual outfit, but somehow, she looked better. Rusty couldn't put a finger to it, but she was looking better every day now. He looked forward to seeing her every morning, to hearing her voice, and even to teasing her. Her hair was combed into an appealing style, curling under with a side part at her bangs and she looked good enough to eat. He took the phone from her and stared at her with a wide grin.

"Rusty, it's Deke. You've got to come home, quick. Can you leave today?"

Rusty was still staring at Hannah and it took a few seconds to regroup his thoughts.

"Well—sure, I guess. What's up?" Rusty's smile faded.

"I'll tell you when you get here and bring Hannah with you."

"Why so mysterious, bro?" Rusty tried to brighten his brother's disposition, but it didn't seem to work.

"Just get back here, and fast."

"Okay, okay, we'll leave tonight."

"Good, see you early morning then."

Hannah took the phone back and looked at him. "Trouble?"

"Don't know." He removed his hat and scratched his head for a second, then readjusted his hat and looked at her. "Deke has a way of being so mysterious at times. He wants me home, and he wants me to bring you..."

"I hope it's nothing serious. But I can't go with you. I've got to take care of things here." She explained.

"Let Burt handle it. He wants us both there."

"What for?"

"Don't know. Just said to be sure and bring you with me."

"I can't just leave...!" She insisted.

"Hannah trust me, if Deke wants you there, it's best."

She frowned then turned her horse around, her movements jerky.

"Where are you going?" Rusty asked as he rode up to her side.

"To let Burt know."

"Why don't you leave that to me."

"But..."

"Please," he said quietly as he kept a steady trot next to her.

"Alright. But I don't see what difference it makes." She cast him a quick frown.

"Yes, you do." Rusty said throatily, smiling slowly, as he stared at her long and hard. His eyes seemed to always land on her mouth and it had Hannah squirming.

Hannah bit her lip and whipped her horse about again to head home.

That evening when Rusty returned to the house Hannah was closing her small overnight bag and she set it in the living room.

He glanced at the bag, then her. "That all you're taking?"

"Isn't it enough?" She gasped.

"I doubt it. We might be a while. It sounded pretty serious to me."

"Well, I can't leave the ranch for that long." A quick flash of anger lit her eyes.

"Take a couple of outfits and the usual stuff women need." He instructed her

Hannah turned to go pack a bigger bag when something dawned on her.

"Did you talk to Burt?"

"I did." His gaze flew over her. "He'll take care of things just fine."

"Any problems?" Her voice sounded unsteady, breathy.

"No, should there be?"

She shrugged. "No, I guess not."

"He wasn't happy about you going with me, if that's what you are getting at." Rusty confessed and seemed to watch her facial expression, for a reaction.

Hannah nodded. "I didn't expect him to be."

"Is there something you want to tell me about Burt and ..."

"No... nothing." She whirled around and stomped back to her bedroom.

Rusty packed his gear and waited while Hannah finished. He threw their bags in the back of the truck when Burt walked up to him.

Just the way he approached him with such haste and determination, told Rusty to be on his guard.

"Something you wanted?"

"Yes sir, there sure as hell is. I been meaning to talk to you for a while now, but I wasn't sure how Hannah would like it." Burt glanced about but didn't see Hannah. "Now, it's time. And it doesn't really matter what Hannah thinks." Burt stood squarely in front of Rusty as though to block him from something.

Rusty knew this wasn't going to go smoothly, he felt the tension that Burt oozed, and he didn't want a scene, but he never walked away from one either. Deke had always warned him that he'd have a showdown.

"Okay, what's up?"

"You can't just haul Hannah out of here. She ain't even married to you yet. It ain't decent. I want you to walk away from this. Right now. I'm askin' you man to man. Walk away. Walk away from this situation and don't look back."

The older man's eyes narrowed on Rusty. "I know she's in trouble. I'll help her."

Rusty eyed the man with new respect. Burt was serious. He really meant what he said, and it was more than obvious he had feelings for Hannah, although Rusty was beginning to doubt the man had ever voiced them to her. The poor old fella was love-sick.

"We're going to my Dad's house for a few days Burt, I don't think that's gonna compromise her." Rusty tried to make light of it.

"Did you hear what I said, I'll help her." Burt's gaze didn't waver.

"Yeah, I heard. But as much as I believe you would, if you could. You can't. She wants to stay here Burt. Her mother is buried here. She won't just up and leave. Don't you see, it's the land? It's in her blood, in the blood of her family. The woman has roots. I'm here to help her, believe it or not. In time this will all settle out and Hannah can do her own choosing, but she's got little choice, she has to keep this land, Burt."

Burt looked curious for a moment as though he weighed Rusty's words.

"Maybe she won't leave, but I can handle it. I'm asking you as a gentleman to walk away from this." Burt came closer. "From her!"

Rusty spread his legs and looked directly at Burt. The silly notion that they must look like a couple of gunfighters during a show-down hit Rusty as comical and he squashed a smile. He knew just how serious Burt was too. "I can't do that. I can't back away. I promised her I'd help her save this place. I aim to do just that."

"You can't, or you won't?" Burt's frown narrowed on him, his mouth set in a grim line.

"Whatever..." Rusty's patience was growing thin.

"You don't love her." Burt burst aloud with his suspicions.

"And you do?" Rusty eyed him closely, noting the way Burt's hands knotted into fists, and stretched as though he were on a tight rope.

"Yes!" The admission flew from Burt's mouth like vile spit.

Rusty started to ignore the situation that was fast becoming heated. He didn't want to fight Burt. He was too old to fight. It'd be like fighting his father. He could never do that. Rusty had the advantage and he knew it. For once he was planning on backing out of a fight.

"I'm sorry Burt, but the lady has made up her mind." Rusty added and started to open the truck door.

"I can't let it happen...I promised her father I'd never let anyone hurt her. And you will. You know you will." Burt said and all of a sudden, he had Rusty by the collar and was laying into him. Rusty didn't bother to counter his blows. Burt had all the advantages simply because Rusty refused to defend himself. He knew what was coming, but he'd rather die than hit a man of Burt's age. Burt on the other hand had no problem and socked him in the jaw. Rusty went down.

Intent on stopping this before it got worse, Rusty stayed down, intentionally.

Hannah came running out of the house. "What are you doing?" She cried and cast a quick scowl at Burt as she bent to check Rusty.

Burt stared at Rusty, then Hannah. "You can't go with him, Hannah. He doesn't love you. You're making a fool of yourself. I can take care of you. You ought to know how I feel about you by now, girl. I can take care of us."

Hannah stepped up to Burt quite suddenly. Her face red from anger, embarrassment and something else. She eyed him closely and her expression was more than serious. "No, you can't Burt. This land is all I have, I won't lose it. I appreciate you're offering, really, I do, but you've gone too far. Rusty doesn't deserve this; he's trying to help me save this place. Can't you understand that?"

Burt frowned and started to argue further. Hannah threw up her hands and shook her head.

"Get your things together and clear out of here."

"You don't mean that...can't mean it." Burt was hurting on the inside, while Rusty still lay slumped against the truck, hurting outside.

"I'm sorry, but I do mean it, Burt. I've told you before I'm not interested in you personally. I tried to be gentle about it. I never wanted to hurt you. I've known you too long to hurt you like this. I should have spoken up sooner. Maybe it would have prevented this. But I knew you just wouldn't listen. I wanted to spare you, but there's just too much age difference. I think of you as an Uncle, not husband material. I'm sorry."

"But..."

She went to Rusty now and cradled his head in her lap, wiping the blood from his mouth with a handkerchief from his back pocket. "Are you alright?"

"Yeah," he said reluctantly, casting a glance at Burt's retreating figure.

Burt shook his head and stalked off, slamming the bunkhouse door as he entered.

A few minutes later Hannah and Rusty were on their way. Rusty blotted his mouth a couple of times and frowned.

The silence in the truck was thick with questions. It was obvious Hannah was upset about firing Burt. And that she didn't want to go with him, but he couldn't understand why. She also didn't want to go with Burt either. She wouldn't have to work, and it might mean a few days of R&R for them both. Why couldn't she just relax?

Rusty settled into the seat comfortably then shot her a glance.

"My family won't eat you alive, Hannah. They're pretty nice when you get to know them."

Hannah sighed heavily, as though she didn't quite believe him. "I'm sure they are."

Rusty's arm went behind her on the seat and she tensed. He smiled to himself. Hannah didn't like him getting close, and it was downright mean to tease her so, but he enjoyed seeing her face turn pink even in the dark. He sensed her emotions. He sensed a lot of things about Hannah, as though he knew her much better and longer than he did.

"Relax, I don't bite either." He said huskily.

"I know..." she sighed again. "I guess I'm just tired." The tension was electrical. "It's been quite a night. I'm sorry about Burt..."

"It was bound to happen, sooner or later."

"That shouldn't have happened, back there," she said a few minutes later.

"I didn't want to hurt him. I didn't want to fight with him."

She nodded as though she knew Rusty had intentionally taken those blows.

"Don't worry about it. I'm just sorry you lost a good hand because of it."

"It was the hardest thing I've ever done in my life. Burt's been like family all these years. He works hard. He's dedicated to the ranch. But..."

"I know," he whispered and took her hand.

This time she didn't jump out of her skin or even act as though she noticed it. She just accepted it.

"Are you hungry?" He asked.

"A little."

"Then we'll stop in town before we leave and get some grub. I'm starving."

She glanced at him. "I should have fixed something at the house."

"There wasn't time for that. But we have to eat, so we'll stop. Okay?"

He looked at her. She glanced at him and the darkness seemed to swallow the moment.

"Okay," came her breathy reply.

During dinner Hannah asked. "Would you mind telling me a little about your family, so I won't be a total idiot when I get there?"

Rusty laughed, and from then on, the conversation poured between them. He told her about his dad, how sick he'd been and how he was finally dating Bertha now. He told her about his brothers and Emma, Abby, and the kids. Hannah seemed interested too. But she was staring at him with a quizzical expression.

"Something wrong?"

"No... well, it's just...well it must be wonderful having a big family like that." She admitted.

"It's pretty nice." He watched her expressions change and smiled.

After a short silence he asked. "Don't you see your brother very often?"

"No, not really. He's been in college, and then when he got out, he began his practice immediately in Arizona and he has very little time off. He married a year ago and they are expecting a child in June. So, the money is pretty tight for him. Jimmy and I are very close, but these days it's a long distance close."

He'd noticed there had been no calls and wondered why a brother so anxious to save the ranch for his sister, couldn't bother with a phone call every now and then. Even when he was away from home a week or two, Deke or Jake or even Clint would call and make sure things were okay and when he'd be home.

"Aren't there any other relatives around?"

"Most of my kinfolks are scattered about the State. Not many left now. A few aunts and uncles and cousins of course. Once a year we have a family reunion, that's about it." She said with a resigned shrug.

"Must get a little lonely." His gaze was curiously intent.

Hannah blushed again, and then concentrated on her food. A few minutes later she admitted, as though his comment needed some clarification. "Yes, it is lonely, sometimes."

"Do you go to these—family reunions?"

"Most of the time, I make an appearance." She smiled shyly.

"Well look, you have no reason to worry about my folks Hannah. They are all a lot like me."

"That's what I'm afraid of," she laughed.

Her laugh was contagious and sexy. He'd never seen her as sexy before, so it stunned him. From then on, he tried to concentrate on his steak and not on how Hannah was affecting him. But it didn't work. Hannah exuded a mysterious kind of charm that Rusty was becoming quite addicted to.

*****

It was nearly dawn when Rusty pulled into the driveway of the 4 Bar None. The fact that the old ranch place looked so good made Rusty feel a certain pride in being a part of it. Even in late winter, the ranch was well manicured, and kept up. Denver the family dog barked and raced about to greet him as usual, while his father came running out to greet them too. Cal's face was masked with a pleasant smile. He seemed eager, and yet there was something bothering him, Rusty could always tell when something bothered his father. There was a certain hesitation in his glance, a weathered frown of worry lined his forehead.

"This is Hannah, dad," Rusty pulled Hannah close to his side possessively and introduced her to his father. He gave Denver a quick pat and obliged him by throwing the toy ball for him that he had brought to Rusty.

"Hannah," Cal repeated, shaking her hand and looking directly into her eyes almost sadly. "I'm pleased to meet you, hon. It's been awhile. Last time I seen you, you were knee high to a grasshopper."

Hannah laughed again, and Rusty found himself aroused by this woman more than he cared to admit. Even her husky laughter seemed to trigger a reaction in him. He didn't understand it. It suddenly struck him how easily Hannah would fit into his life and family, and that knowledge stunned him too. Why was he thinking about Hannah in such a permanent way? They both knew and accepted that this was only temporary.

"Where's Deke?" he asked drawing his attention purposely away from Hannah.

"He's nursin' a sick calf in the barn. He'll be in directly. Come on in, Hannah and have some of Emma's biscuits and gravy."

Hannah nodded and followed them in, slinking away from Rusty's possessive hold of her.

Rusty moved closer, determined not to leave her side. Rusty wanted to get to the bottom of the mystery though. His father was evading the issue.

"Maybe I better go out and see him," Rusty said as Hannah followed him into the house.

"Don't bother, he'll be in directly. Let's get some grub and get Hannah settled in, first." Cal frowned at his son as though he'd forgot his manners.

"Yeah, sure."

Emma came out of the hallway and greeted them with a child on her hip and one at her side. Without missing a step, she swiped Rusty's cheek with a sisterly kiss and smiled at Hannah. She was dressed in jeans and sweatshirt, and her hair was tied back in a ponytail. Hannah knew she was a ranch-girl just from the way she handled herself.

"You must be Hannah, I'm Emma. These little rascals are mine. Come on in, I've got breakfast hot on the stove."

Hannah seemed surprised at how friendly the Travers bunch were, accepting her as almost family immediately.

Rusty eyed Emma as she put fresh butter on the biscuits and waited until she brought them to the table before asking. "So, what's the emergency?"

Emma shot him a quick reprimand. "You'll have to ask Deke."

Why was everyone being so evasive? Deke had called him home, why couldn't someone tell him why?

Rusty thought about his current situation, wondering if he'd done something to annoy his brother or anyone else in the family. Deke didn't sound very happy on the phone and he couldn't begin to imagine what had gone wrong.

Hannah only ate a few bites before pushing her plate away. Rusty sensed her unease and insisted she could eat more than that.

"I'm really not very hungry, haven't done any work to make me," she tried to smile but it fell short and Rusty knew she was a quivering mass. He wanted to comfort her, reassure her, but he knew she'd have to learn to take the Travers bunch as they were. Instead he grabbed her hand under the table and squeezed it, communicating silently that he understood, and it would be alright.

Half an hour later, Rusty was showing Hannah his prize championship stock, as they lingered in the meadow. Each and every one of them were perfect, Hannah acknowledged. Prize stock! Hannah shook her head, as she leaned on the gate. "I don't blame you for not wanting to put those up for collateral. I'm not sure I would do such a thing, in your place."

"I don't intend to lose them, Hannah."

She glanced at him and he winked. He put his arm around her and led her back to the house where Emma was feeding the baby. Deke strolled into the kitchen, his expression almost grim as he shook hands with Hannah and nodded to his brother. Rusty noticed the tension in his brother's walk and stance. This couldn't be good news.

Ordinarily he would have grabbed his brother for a hug. Something was definitely wrong.

"Okay, spit it out, what's up?" Rusty demanded, not waiting a moment later.

Deke glanced at him with a frown, then at Hannah. "We'll talk about it later." Deke tried to stall as he took over the chore of feeding his youngest.

Just the look in Deke's eyes should have told Rusty to be quiet, but he seemed determined to get to the bottom of the mystery. Rusty shook his head. "If it's that bad, we'd better get to it now."

Deke sighed, had Emma pour him a cup of coffee and told the children to go wash their hands. He eyed Hannah for a long moment, as though sizing her up and the situation between his brother and her. "I think we should discuss this in private, bro."

Rusty eyed him, then everyone else. Hannah sat with her hand still in his, and her head bowed as though melting under the table and out of sight.

"Anything you have to say, can be said in front of Hannah, after all, we're gonna be married soon. Besides, it was you that insisted she come too."

Deke firmed his lips and frowned again. Bad choice, Rusty guessed.

"All right. I suppose she is entitled to know. There's just no easy way to put this, for either of you. So, I'm just gonna spit it out...Jennifer is back!"

# Chapter Seven

There was a long silence, as though everyone at the table held their breath. Hannah included.

Like a steam engine suddenly running out of steam, Rusty sat very still. He'd expected anything but that! Outside he looked calm, but inside he was churning with questions, and anger.

He wasn't comfortable talking about this in front of Hannah.

Fool, he chided himself silently. Why couldn't he have waited for Deke to talk to him later? Why did he have to act like some kid who couldn't wait to hear the news? For all the world he wouldn't hurt Hannah, but this...

Jennifer! He'd never thought she'd come back. In fact, he hated to admit it, but Jennifer hadn't been on his mind lately. It boggled his mind, screwed his thinking and made him angry all at the same time. Why in hell did his brother insist on Hannah coming with him, then? Angrier with his brother, than anyone, Rusty looked for some outlet for all the emotions crowding him.

Hannah started to get up from the table and excuse herself, but Rusty was having none of that. He pulled her hand closer to him and sat very still as he eyed Deke first, then his father who looked white as a ghost.

"Stay Hannah. I want you to stay." Rusty said with a steel edge to his voice.

"Okay," she whispered.

"You brought me back home, for this?" he demanded from Deke some sort of explanation.

Deke began to fidget some as Emma sat the plate of biscuits in front of Deke with a decided frown. At least Emma understood how awkward this was.

Without a doubt Deke seemed confident he'd done the right thing. "I had to, bro. I'm the one that forced you into this." He shot Hannah a quick apologetic glance. "I thought it only fair to give you a choice. No offense Hannah, this isn't your fault. I'm sorry I had to broadcast it like this."

"None taken," Hannah rushed to say. Although she had been shy when she first walked in, she suddenly seemed to take the bull by the horns. Obviously, she saw and understood the awkward position everyone was in.

"Deke's right, Rusty. You'd have never forgiven him if he'd kept it from you."

How did she know that? How did she know anything? And yet she did. She seemed so wise to him suddenly, so mature and capable of handling anything, something else to like about Hannah.

"You never should have called me Deke, it's of no importance," Rusty insisted, standing up and pulling Hannah along with him. "Emma you got a room ready for Hannah. We've been in the truck all night, and I'm sure she needs some rest."

Emma nodded and cast her husband another frown. "Well, don't look at me that way Emma. I was only thinking of Rusty." Deke managed as everyone stared at him.

"I appreciate your concern, bro. Really, but Hannah and me will be getting married this weekend, here!" Rusty announced.

"This weekend...?"

Hannah jerked loose of his hold and put her hands on her hips. "Your brother was trying to do the right thing by you. Giving you a chance. As he should for shoving this whole situation down your throat. I'd think the least you could do would be to see Jennifer and find out how you feel about her...before the wedding."

Rusty glared at her now. "I don't need to see Jennifer. She left me, remember?" He shouted.

"That's male ego talking." Hannah replied huskily.

Emma took Hannah by the arm and led her down the hall and away from the men who were making a mess of it. "Let's leave it for now, and get you comfortable, hon. I'm sure you are exhausted."

"I am a little tired," Hannah sighed, obviously glad to be out of that line of fire.

Rusty ranted and raved for several minutes, then stomped out of the house.

Hannah watched from the window as he walked down the long pathway leading to the pastures. Her entire fate was in his hands and right now all she could think about was how much she might mess his life up...

*****

That afternoon Hannah was standing by the kitchen door staring out when Emma came in and began preparing the evening meal. As she worked, she'd glance at Hannah, and finally she broached the subject.

"Hannah, I'm sorry about all this."

"No need to be. Deke did right."

"Yes, but dragging you here, wasn't such a great idea."

"Maybe, maybe it was. At least he didn't do it behind my back. I'm rather grateful for that."

"Then you do understand."

"Of course. Rusty loves Jennifer, he's just too stubborn to admit it. At least this way he has a chance to right the wrongs."

Emma stopped cleaning the vegetables and looked at her. "What a very good person you are Hannah. I'm so pleased to meet you. In other circumstances, I'm sure Rusty would fall in love with you."

Hannah frowned, glancing down at her clothes that she intentionally wore to ward men out of her life, she suddenly almost regretted it. Would Rusty have fallen in love with her if she'd have worn different clothes, worn make-up? It didn't matter, that was a frivolous kind of love and she wanted no part of it.

"I think it's terribly romantic. Rusty loves her dearly, and I'm wearing the proof."

"What do you mean." Emma asked.

"Look," she extended her hand, so Emma could see the ring. Emma gasped.

"Oh my..." Emma's hand went to her mouth as she gaped at the diamond.

Hannah smiled sadly. "Yes, the minute he gave it to me, I realized he loved someone very much. He told me about her."

"He did?" Emma seemed surprised.

Hannah nearly laughed. "He thought we should get to know one another since we were going to get married."

"And still might."

"No, I wouldn't hold him to that. In fact, I think I'll leave early in the morning, if you don't mind. I need to get back. I just fired my foreman and I'm needed there."

"But Hannah..." Emma protested.

"Please don't say anything to Rusty. I'd rather just leave it at that, if you don't mind. I can't tell you all how much I appreciate the offer to help, but under these circumstances, I just can't accept."

Emma started to protest, but Hannah's expression stopped her. "Okay Hannah. We owe you that much."

"Thanks." Hannah sighed with relief, then began helping Emma prepare the meal as though she'd been part of the family for years. Surprisingly the conversation flowed between them in the same manner. Hannah liked Emma, she liked Rusty's family. And a small part of her felt sad to not be a part of it. But that was silly. She didn't belong here, she told herself silently.

She kept telling herself that when the conversation at supper flowed naturally between herself and his family.

Rusty had been unusually quiet, but Hannah understood his silence.

After dishes were done, she donned her jacket and walked outside. It was cold, but there was a full moon and a beautiful night. Hannah walked for a long while, thinking over her options. She could go back to Vegas, and eventually earn enough to buy the ranch back, or at least the graveyard. What use would strangers have for a graveyard?

Yes, as much as she hated wearing those costumes and parading up and down those stages, it paid good money. Better than any regular job. And she could find a place of her own and begin again, anew!

Just as she had all her thoughts arranged and just as she was about to turn around and go back to the house, a horse and rider came up to her.

"Where have you been?" Rusty's cool tone broke her musings, as he swung down off the saddle. There was a note of concern in his voice that had her staring.

"Walking, why?" She asked as her voice faded into the darkness.

"It's too cold to be out here." He objected coming closer and draping an arm over her shoulders, as though it were a natural thing for him to do.

"A little, but it's a beautiful night, though." She said and glanced up at the stars in the sky, ignoring that slight spark of electricity that always connected them. "They look almost touchable, don't they?"

"What...?" His voice grew husky as he seemed to pull her closer into the circle of his arms.

"The stars." She gestured, needing to put space between those comfortable warm arms he offered.

"Yeah, I guess." He glanced down at her, and his breath hitched as she stared into his eyes, reaching into her heart and reading her thoughts. Hannah's eyes were so expressive. "Now listen Hannah. We need to talk."

"About...?" Her voice was a mere hushed whisper.

"About us." He met her gaze and the intensity made her look away. Why did she have the urge to run into his arms and never let go?

"There is no us, Rusty." She insisted trying to pull away, but he was having none of that. He kept her tucked against him.

She stopped resisting and took a deep breath about to continue her explanation.

"Isn't there?" he reached down to touch her cheek with his knuckles. It was a simple act, but it was so gentle, so very comforting, her cheek seemed to soak it up. Gently stroking he watched her, fascinated that her eyes seemed to speak for her. Her dark eyes danced with life and so much more.

She almost backed away like a skittish kitten but backing away would be admitting he was getting to her, and he was, he decided with a satisfied smile.

He slowly turned her toward him, his head bent, and she sensed his kiss that never came. His hot gaze swept over her, but instead he smiled gently at her as though having second thoughts about his reactions. Then he guided her toward his horse. "Let's get back, Emma's worried about you."

"I'm sorry." The spell was broken, and she did back away from him then.

"We were all worried." He quickly amended. He hoisted her up and into his saddle, then slid up behind her, so that his arms were around her.

A sudden warmth surrounded them. She tensed. Being this close to him did things to her. Things she didn't want to think about. She felt her own heartbeat quicken. She smelled the fresh woodsy cologne he wore, felt the smooth of his cheek. Everything inside her seemed to melt at once, yet she still managed to create a false front for him.

His cheek grazed hers. She held her breath for a moment, trying to release the tension inside her as she calmed her nerves and reserve. She closed her eyes and willed herself to sit straight and not yield to the power of this man's charms. She felt her own cheeks grow hot. Her breath caught in her throat. Plain and simple desire, squelched only by her determination, threatened to surface. If she turned her head, he'd kiss her, she knew it, but she refused the glory of it. Even though every muscle strained silently toward him, she resisted. His lips would taste warm, and a shiver ran through her encouraging her to invite the kiss. Her mind said one thing, her body another and she was at war with the odds.

Instead she sat stiffly in place, as the warmth of his body surrounded her. It was the hardest thing she had ever done. Wanting a man, this desperately, had never been a part of her life, until now. But now was not the time, this was not the place, and Rusty, was not the man, she decided with deep regret. She felt like a mirror cracking open into a million different pieces. Shattering from a need so buried inside her she hadn't known it was there.

Every movement seemed to bring them closer. Every thrust of the saddle brought an awareness. Had he thrown her to the ground and made wild passionate love to her, she would not have felt it any deeper, closer, or more vividly. He was making love to her. Cowboy love! She smelled the distinct odor that was all Rusty, she felt the power in his arms, felt the tense, taut muscles of his shoulders and chest. She also felt the security of being wrapped in those arms, and totally protected. For a brief moment she almost weakened and turned into him, but stiffening her resolve, she never let it happen. It would be too hurtful to fall for this cowboy. If it wasn't already too late...

Just as they reached the yard, he pulled her solidly against him. An immediate tension swept between them. Her heart leapt, knowing full well he was just as distraught this moment as she. She felt the fast, hard beat of his heart. It matched her own. Again, her breath hitched, her glance slid slowly to his through the darkness, and the heat of the moment nearly consumed them. For just a second, she relaxed, her body melting against his into one pool of pent up longing. She closed her eyes, savored the moment, knowing that one turn would have her consenting to this silent love-making. Her back was hard against his chest and shoulders now. Her head was mere inches from his and his lips began to descend, slowly with purpose. She felt his hot breath against her temple. Suddenly, he pulled her hard against him, so that only clothes separated them and kept their sanity. She felt the rise of desire in him and gasped. His hands went slowly down her arms then he wrapped them under her breast and set her on his thigh, so he could see her face. This was the moment she'd waited for, the moment she had denied herself. But there was no denying what they both wanted at this moment, it was in their eyes as they gazed into each other's faces, it was in their heartbeat as they melted into the embrace, it was in the heat of the moment that sanity fled, and feelings took over. The gentle rock of the horse beneath them merely emphasized their needs. Never had Hannah felt such a pull toward a man. As though her body and mind had no control. As though coming together was all that mattered in the world. In that moment, Hannah knew she'd give him anything.... anything.

And then...a porch light came on, and she jerked upright and back to sanity.

"Oh good, you found her." Emma called in a worried tone.

Hannah reddened at the thought of what she almost let happen. On top a horse, for God's sake, had she lost her mind? So close and yet so far. Rusty was here to be reunited with his old love, his true love and here she had nearly let the unthinkable happen between them. What was wrong with her? She'd never been this close to losing it all with a man. Never wanted a man in such a way. Shame clouded the glory of what they might have had.

She couldn't allow herself to love this cowboy. Wouldn't! It would be fatal to her heart! But somewhere deep inside her heart...she knew it was too late.

And with that firmly implanted in her head she jumped out of his arms and ran for the house. She didn't look back, didn't explain her hasty retreat to safety. She couldn't.

"Did I interrupt something?" Emma asked as she watched Hannah run.

"N-no, nothing that won't keep." Rusty replied his voice faltering from a whisper to a rough rasping.

Deke joined them on the porch. "Jennifer's coming over in the morning."

"What for?" Rusty demanded, disoriented from the conversation by his own welling need of Hannah. What had just happened? What was wrong with him? The only thing he wanted at this moment was to excuse himself from his well-intentioned brother and sister-in- law and chase after Hannah to explain.... or to finish making love to her, if she still wanted him as much as he did her.

But explain what? How could he explain the white-hot heat that had surfaced so fast and furious between them? And he was sure of one thing, it hadn't been one sided. He knew when a woman wanted him. Trouble was...he wanted her too!

"To see you I guess." Deke replied twisting his head in one of those questioning Travers gazes.

"Did you tell her I wanted to see her?" Rusty tried to get hold of himself, tried to bring his mind back to the conversation, but his body wasn't willing. It'd be almost impossible to dismount and walk away right now, so he stayed atop the horse.

"Not exactly." Deke cast him another strange look.

"What time..." Rusty squirmed.

"I don't know, I guess after breakfast." Deke glanced at Emma, and when Emma shot him a look of 'leave him alone', they went inside the house.

Rusty dismounted slowly a few minutes later, willing himself under control as he led the horse back to the barn. After feeding and combing him, he decided to clean the stall. He just couldn't go to bed yet. Mainly because he couldn't put away those strange and wonderful feelings. He'd never gone through anything like that before.

An hour later he paced the porch, his boots making a loud thunder of their own. His anger festered. Jennifer. Of all times for her to show up. Now what was he going to do? And what about Hannah. Why had he had this strange sexual pull toward her? How embarrassing this must be for her. Why did Deke insist on him bringing her? Even though he didn't love Hannah he didn't want to hurt her. He liked her too much to hurt her. And he would have to get his lust under control too, because the last thing he wanted was to hurt her.

And what about Jennifer? Did she expect him to just forgive her and things go back to normal? He wasn't even sure what normal was anymore.

What kind of man was he? How could he have been so turned on by Hannah with this turn of events? Nothing like that had ever happened to him before. The feelings were more intense than if he'd taken her. He'd never felt such an intense need of a woman before. Jennifer had teased and taunted him, but she'd never made his blood boil and his heart pound so loud it sounded as though it might burst right through his chest.

What was it about Hannah?

He headed for the kitchen and poured himself a big glass of milk, which he downed in a second. Then he poured another.

Cal walked in and smiled sadly.

"Well now boy, looks like you got problems."

Rusty nodded. "And then some."

"Well, don't be too hard on Deke. He had your best interest at heart. He knows how much you loved Jennifer. It's only fair to give you a second chance.... if you want it. Guilt made him call you, Rusty."

Rusty glanced at his father, who looked better now than he had three years ago, before he quit smoking. Before Sammie Jo came into his life and ignited a new glow inside him. Rusty smiled to himself. How did women manage to do that, he wondered? How could they take a man and change him almost over-night?

"Right now, I'm not sure what I want, Dad."

Cal shook his head and poured himself a glass of milk. "Yeah, I figured as much. Hannah's a nice young lady."

"She really is."

"You like her, don't you?"

"Yeah, I do."

"And what about Jennifer?"

"I don't know. She can't just waltz back into my life and say it doesn't matter, Dad. It does. She walked out. Without a word. That's not love..."

His father smiled strangely. "And are you now an expert on love?"

"Hell no! I'm not even sure what it is, anymore." He downed his second glass of milk and wiped his white mustache as Cal gave him a grin.

Cal twisted his head. "You know, sometimes people need some space to see what they really want."

Rusty glanced at him again. "Or don't want."

"Or don't want." Cal smiled, and stood up, putting his hand on Rusty's shoulder.

"Just make sure you know what you *do* want." Cal said starting to leave.

"Dad, can I ask you something?" Rusty hesitated, looking at his father closely.

"Sure," Cal said returning to the table and glancing down into Rusty's solemn face.

"Have you ever wanted a woman so bad...you sorta lost control...of yourself?" Rusty asked, his voice low and thoughtful.

"Many times." Cal chuckled.

"What makes a man that way?" Rusty asked.

"With me, it was your mother, son. She could make me want her in the strangest places and at the strangest times." Cal nodded, as though it was a mystery to him too, as though he could conjure his beautiful dead wife up at a moment's notice.

"Really, was it just Mom, or was it all the women you knew?" Rusty asked.

Cal shook his head, "No, no one could do that to me, but your mother, son. She had a fire about her that I never saw in other women."

Rusty nodded. "A fire. Is that what it is? Was Mom beautiful?"

"Beautiful?" Cal's head twisted, and he sat down in the chair opposite Rusty and looked at his son, and then a slow, sad smile lit his face. "Son, maybe against other women, she wasn't exactly cover girl material, but when I looked into her eyes, and saw the light there, I just didn't see other women anymore. There was something about her. Whether it was her smile, that was slow and burning, her eyes that danced when she talked, her voice, kinda throaty, I don't know what it was, but I never wanted another woman after I met her. So yes, I guess she was just about the most beautiful woman I'd ever seen."

Rusty seemed completely spellbound by his father's words. He listened and then stood up and grabbed his father's shoulder. "Thanks Dad. It's nice to hear you talk about Mom, again."

"Maybe I should have talked to you more about her, son. You didn't get a chance to know her. I know you've been carrying the guilt all these years. It wasn't your fault you know. I never blamed you. She wanted you more than her own life. If she could have chosen, she would have chosen your life over hers any day. That's the way she was, the kind of woman she was."

Rusty listened intently, soaking up the information like a sponge. Then he laid a quick hand on his dad's shoulder and stood up.

Cal stared at his son then nodded. "Night son."

"Night dad," Rusty called watching his father walk away, a new and deeper understanding of the man he called Dad suddenly on his shoulders…

*****

The next morning Rusty knocked on Hannah's door and there was no answer. Slowly he turned the knob and peeked in. Hannah and her bag were gone.

Rusty stomped loudly to the kitchen. "Hannah's not in her bedroom."

Emma nodded as she stirred the gravy. "She went home, Rusty."

"Home?" he boomed.

"Said she just fired her foreman and was needed. Sounded reasonable to me. After all, she does have a ranch to run."

"Reasonable? She's gone!" He repeated as though his brain was still fuzzy, and he couldn't quite think.

"Did you know she fired her foreman?"

Rusty glanced away from the all-knowing look on Emma's face. "Yeah, that's my problem, I know a little about a lot."

"Maybe it's for the best, hon. You don't need an audience when Jennifer comes, now do you?" Emma's sympathy was showing and Rusty realized she only wanted to help.

Rusty looked around the table at all the questions on everyone else's faces. "I guess not. But she could have at least told me she was leaving."

"I guess I put her in an embarrassing position." Deke admitted as he sipped his coffee and didn't quite meet Rusty's glance.

"You sure as hell did that, bro." Rusty frowned. He wanted to slam his fist on the table, he wanted to break something. He wanted out of this mess. He'd never felt out of control before, but right now, he wasn't sure what to do about it.

"For that, I'm sorry. But doing it behind her back didn't seem right either. Better she knows up front, then...later."

"Know what?" Rusty demanded.

"Well, everybody knows you're going to go back to Jennifer, after you forgive her." Deke said almost grudgingly, as though he didn't particularly cotton to the idea, but accepted it as fact.

"Yeah? Who said."

"Well....aren't you?" Deke's eyebrow raised a hair as he stared at his brother in disbelief.

Rusty stood up from the table, glanced at them all, one by one. "I don't know..."

# Chapter Eight

The north wind whistled through the barn door like a siren from a police car. It's cold and lonely sound ripping at Hannah's heart. Hannah tried to ignore it. She pulled her gloves on and began distributing the hay about the stalls. Methodically she groomed the horses, until their coats shined, and they neighed their approval. Hannah hardly noticed.

She heard Pepper barking from the doorway, where she had deliberately left him. At least he wanted to console her. He'd been by her side since she arrived, as though he knew there was something troubling her.

She hadn't warmed up a bit. The wind's song was little comfort, one she wouldn't dwell on, she told herself. Pulling her coat tighter she stomped her booted feet to get some feeling back into them. Pulling her jacket closer about her, she tried not to shiver from the invading cold.

She'd spent an hour chipping ice in the watering holes. Even though she'd worn gloves her hands were raw and freezing. Hard work was good for what ailed her, she decided. Maybe if she froze, she'd numb the feelings running through her now. Feelings she tried to squash in every other way and failed.

She couldn't help reliving that moment on the horse with Rusty. It scared her, and yet the feelings that had swamped her still made her swoon. Never had any man affected her that way, so intently. So much so she forgot who and where she was. Every fiber of her being had wanted to be one with Rusty. Perhaps she should be ashamed of that, but for some reason she couldn't be. It had felt as though God Almighty had put them together.

As though it was meant to be. How could anything that wonderful be so wrong?

And yet so right!

She'd just have to file it away in her heart as a precious memory, because that's all it would ever be for her.

Reality told her Rusty was going back to Jennifer.

She should be cussing the Travers bunch for involving her in Rusty's reunion. Yet, it was better knowing what was going on, and not being shocked later. Although him going back to Jennifer shouldn't be such a shock, her mind tried to reason. She had thought all along he would do just that. So why did she feel so lost all of a sudden? So, surprised at her own heartache?

She shook her head vehemently. How could a woman fall so hard?

She wasn't going to think about Rusty anymore. She couldn't. Truth be known, she'd come to like Rusty a little too much for comfort. A lot too much! And despite the marriage that never happened, Hannah couldn't stop the feeling of loss that had swamped her on her return home. It was utter nonsense to miss someone she barely knew. And yet, despite the amount of time she'd spent with Rusty, she felt she did know him. He was a rancher, much like herself. He knew his work, spoke his mind, and lived the true life of a cowboy. Even went as far as living by the cowboy code of ethics.

She thought she'd feel better when she was surrounded by her home and land, but this time, she felt empty. As empty as when her father had died, and she'd come home to a barren house. The stark reality of being alone again sent another shiver through her.

She pulled the flop hat down and grabbed the pitch fork.

She'd never forget that forlorn loneliness that hit her when she walked through the door of the ranch house and realized finally that her father was truly dead.

Leaving the ranch and her father had been hard, but her reasoning behind it solid. She had to make some money, somehow. She had to help her father keep this ranch, it meant too much to them. However, her leaving for Vegas nearly broke her father's heart. She'd never stepped foot out of Texas before. She'd witnessed the heartbreak in his eyes. Still, she had to help him keep his dream and Jimmy's too.

Pepper stood up on the door and it opened enough for him to slip through the crack. He ran up to her and nudged her leg for a pat. Hannah smiled and felt the tears welling. Even Pepper wasn't hers, and she had come to love him too!

She scoffed at herself and flung a big teardrop away as she continued working. Tears! She couldn't remember the last time she'd cried. She hadn't cried when she buried her father, she couldn't. She was too empty. She hadn't cried when she found Vic in bed with her roommate, again only an emptiness. But now...a tear!

"You forgot something, didn't you?" A sultry voice from behind her, startled her.

Dear God, it couldn't be him? How could she face him? She'd just flicked a tear away. He'd see she'd been crying. But pride held her still for a moment as she gained control. She stood ramrod straight, willing a calm she didn't feel. Hannah stopped pitching hay and slowly turned around to face Rusty staring hard and not too happily at her.

Pepper nudged him for a pat.

"At least someone's glad to see me." Rusty chuckled as he bent to pet the dog.

Puzzled by his question and wondering why he'd come here, she frowned. Why did he have to come back, her mind screamed. She hadn't wanted to say goodbye. She wasn't sure she could. Looking so damned handsome standing there with that big frown on his face, she had an urge to run into his arms and hug him close. Still, she would have gotten over him in time. "So, what did I forget?" Was that her voice that quivered so?

He stuck the ring out in front of her, and she gazed at the beautiful diamond that beckoned her attention. She'd left it on the pillow in the room she'd slept in last night. She loved that ring, had dreams about it. It was perhaps the only material thing other than her land that she had come to cherish. But it wasn't hers, and she knew it.

"That's not mine and you know it, Rusty." She said moving to turn away from him.

Rusty was having none of that, he followed and stepped in front of her. He grabbed her hand, and slid it on her finger, even though she tried to resist.

"You're freezing, what are you doing out here this time of night?"

"This is a ranch, we work 24/7 here, and you know that." She declared glancing at the ring momentarily and wishing with all her might that she didn't love the feel of it on her finger. "The water froze up, I had to chip it. Things have to be done. I'm doing them."

"As I recall we had a wedding to attend."

Hannah dropped the pitch fork and looked up at him. A big mistake. Her heart leapt at seeing his face, but she quickly masked her reactions. It'd be foolish to fall for this man, she scolded herself silently.

She put her hands on her hips and frowned instead. "Now look, Rusty..."

"No....you look lady." He came closer his eyes were trained on her, but his voice softened. "We're engaged, officially, in front of witnesses. In case you've forgotten. And no matter what my brother thinks about my past. He's forgotten one thing."

"And what is that?" Hannah snapped.

"I said I would help you keep this place, Hannah, I meant it." Rusty said eyeing her as though testing his own words. His face was solemn.

He did mean it. And damn if she didn't love him for that!

Hannah stared at the man in disbelief. What had happened between him and Jennifer? Had she rejected him, again? Or was this some noble gesture on his part to keep his word? She knew his ethics were unquestionable, yet, his reasons might hold concern.

"Under the circumstances...."

"There are no circumstances, we're getting married, Hannah. Tomorrow, so get yourself a dress, and whatever else you need and let's do it."

Hannah didn't like his assertiveness. Why was he suddenly so set on marrying her now? Perhaps Jennifer had dumped him, and he wanted revenge. That made sense.

"I'm not wearing a dress, and I'm not getting married." She said determined to make him see sense.

"Fine, don't wear a dress. I don't care if you get married in your birthday suit, but come morning, at ten o'clock we are gonna be married."

He turned then and started marching toward the barn door.

She ran after him, trying to pull the ring from her finger, but it seemed stuck. Giving up with that, she began pulling him around by the arm.

"Wait just a minute, I don't know what happened back there, with you and Jennifer, but this is insanity. Under the circumstances, I won't marry you."

His eyes narrowed on her, his stance was that of a gunfighter facing his enemy. But his face was all smiles now. "Little darlin', we better get one thing straight, right now. I'm the straw boss around here and what I say goes. The animals respect it, the men have learned it, and you...my little lady will too. And I say we're getting married—tomorrow!"

Perhaps she needed to take a new tack with him. "But what about Jennifer? There's no reason to torture her so. I'll find another way..."

"There is no other way. Now," his eyes seemed to soften on her now, as though he suddenly liked looking at her.

What that gaze did to her heart beat was frightening. She couldn't fall for a man that was in love with another woman...not again. She couldn't be that foolish...again!

His finger reached to gently stoke her cheek, creating a hot flush to her face. "Be ready at ten, in your living room, we have guests coming."

"Guests? Who...?"

"My family for one, some of the locals around here and the ranch hands and their families. And the banker."

"But how..."

"I've been on the phone ever since I packed and left the house. I'll have one helluva phone bill, but it will be worth it."

Hannah stared with huge brown eyes up at him. "But we can't do this. Rusty you aren't thinking straight right now. Not that I blame you. You've had a shock."

"I'm thinking very straight. And we can, and we will."

Then he was gone, and Pepper followed barking with obvious joy to see his master.

*****

Rusty went into the ranch house, turned on the heat, lit a fire, and went to shower. He was dead tired, but glad he'd come. Hannah had all but given up on him. So, had his family. Hell, he wasn't sure why he was doing this, himself. He wasn't sure why seeing Hannah's face made him so happy either. But it did. The strangest part was why he'd sent Jennifer on her way. Only, he'd realized as soon as he saw Jennifer that whatever he'd felt for her, whatever they had once was gone. Over.

It was a relief to know. Jennifer had toyed with his affections for too long, and truth be known, he'd fallen for her for the wrong reasons. He knew that now. When she drove up in his drive with her sporty new Porsche, got out in her fancy clothes and beauty parlor hair, he suddenly realized how shallow a man he was. It hit him like a tornado. He hadn't loved Jennifer. Love wasn't a pretty body and curves. It ran deeper than that. At least he thought it was. It had to do with liking a person...a lot. It had to do with enjoying the small things in life, not the big things.

Love was about feelings, honesty, knowing someone so well that you could second guess them. Love was all that and more.

Strange how at home he suddenly felt here. He smiled and whistled as he showered, knowing the floor was gonna be cold when he stepped out. But that fire he'd lit in the fireplace would feel good.

He thought about how surprised Jennifer had been when he didn't kiss her. Surprised when he didn't act glad to see her. And how he almost felt an odd pity for her now. Beautiful yes, but not for him. He wanted more than a package, a pretty figure. He wanted a woman. He wanted a woman who would stand by his side, through thick and thin. Like Emma had with Deke, and Abby had with Clint. Jennifer was still the little cheer-leader he'd grown up with. She hadn't matured. And he suddenly realized—he had!

He smiled and whistled as he shaved and combed his hair, then wrapped a towel around himself and headed for the bedroom. His bedroom! At least the one he'd picked out as his.

Just as he came through the door, Hannah nearly ran into him.

He reached out to grab her, and she bolted away when she realized he wasn't wearing his jeans.

"I... I'm sorry. I didn't know...I mean." she stammered, and her face flushed again.

Her hands were still cold, but she'd moved as if he'd burnt her. He smiled.

"Thought I'd get in there tonight as I'm sure you'll need it in the morning, right?"

She shook her head, as though clearing it. "We need to talk."

"Mind if I get some clothes on first, it's a little chilly this way." He glanced down, and she flushed again. He liked that flush. Yes siree, there were a lot of things he was beginning to like about Hannah.

"Of course, I'll make us some hot chocolate." She began backing away.

"How about a big bowl of popcorn to go with it?" He suggested with a wink.

She gulped and nodded, but not before her glance took him all in. The slow rate her eyes traveled over him, made him grin.

Rusty smiled at her hasty retreat too, knowing full well she was embarrassed at being caught gawking. Again, thoughts of whether she might be a virgin flitted through his mind, this time he didn't dismiss them. This time he pondered about Hannah even further. He didn't know much about her life, but he intended to find out.

He threw on a pair of red checkered pajama bottoms. He was tying the pajamas as he walked into the living room. Pepper had already found his place by the fire and was nearly asleep.

Going to the fire, he waited for her to join him, and then he sat in the recliner and put on a pair of socks to keep his feet warm. He had put his hat on, force of habit he reckoned, and let it lie.

Hannah hadn't changed clothes yet, but if she had ideas to go back out in this cold, he'd soon change them for her. She didn't know it yet, but for a while, he was taking over.

A few minutes later Hannah brought a tray of hot chocolate and a big bowl of popcorn and placed it on the coffee table. At first glance, she nearly dropped the tray. The man was lethal with those pajamas riding low on his hips, and no shirt and a cowboy hat on his head. What a picture he made. What a big lovable picture.

She sat down stiffly, her eyes flitting all over him and away. It was obvious she wasn't comfortable, and her eyes seemed to stray to his pajamas more than once.

"This looks great. Want to watch TV?" he suggested as though he had no idea, she was uncomfortable. He sorta liked the way she squirmed.

"You can, I've got to get back to the barn." She began and started to get up again.

He shook his head, as his hand extended to stay her. "No, you don't, young lady. It's too cold to be out there any more than is necessary. Now relax, cover up and let's share a minute. After all, we are getting married tomorrow."

"Rusty," she began, but he held up his finger to her lips and winked.

"I know you've got questions, and I'll be glad to answer them, in time." He said.

She leaned back into the couch and stared at him a long time. He didn't mind that she was looking at much more than his face now. In fact, he rather enjoyed it, but he wished he could see a little more than those baggy clothes she wore too. In fact, his curiosity was getting the best of him. What was she hiding, a thick waist, or a little pot belly? It couldn't be much. He'd been on top of her and hadn't noticed any bulges in the wrong direction. Maybe she was one of those shy little creatures that just didn't know how pretty she was.

He crossed his long legs, pushed back his hat and dug into the popcorn, trying to squash his own curiosity.

After a few minutes she took off her boots and tucked her feet under her as she pulled the afghan over her. When she had almost warmed up, and her eyes began to droop a little he smiled.

"That's better isn't it?"

She shot him a scowl. "Yes, but don't think I'm taking orders from you all the time."

"No ma'am." His teasing smile smoothed her frown away.

"Are you going to tell me what happened?"

He put his hot chocolate down and leaned back into the recliner. "Not much."

He saw her eyes flash with anger and he smiled. "Okay. Jennifer came to the house this morning. She had a brand-new car, new clothes, and a great job. In the city of course. She was happy, she said."

"And..."

"I'm getting there." He grinned. "Nothing happened. I took one look and it hit me.... I wasn't in love with her."

Hannah straightened and glared at him, narrowing her pretty brown eyes on him like a dog ready to pounce.

"Oh God," she rolled her eyes. "Men are so shallow. How can you suddenly be out of love with someone? Especially someone you've been involved with for years."

"I don't know." He shrugged, as though it had perplexed him too, popping the popcorn into his mouth and glancing at her again. "Unless maybe I wasn't in love with her in the first place. I just know that I looked at her and felt absolutely nothing for her. Except maybe pity."

"Pity?"

Rusty stared at Hannah a minute, looking straight into those warm brown eyes that were so expressive, he could almost read her every thought. "She's found a great paying job, got all those fancy things she always wanted, and says she's happy."

"Then why pity her?"

Rusty looked down at the floor for a minute, reflecting on the day. "Because when I looked at her, I saw me, a few months ago. And I didn't like what I saw. I measured Jennifer by her looks, her ambition, and her place in society. I put all my opinions in who she was, what she was, not what was in here..." He pointed to his heart. "Not what is really important about a person. What makes that person special?"

What he said must have had some impact because Hannah's eyes softened on him.

"Most men do..."

"Do what?"

"Measure a woman by her looks."

"Well...not me...not anymore. I see how shallow it all is now. Don't ask me how I see it, suddenly. I just do. I took a long hard look at myself and decided I didn't like me very much. And I'll bet Jennifer doesn't like herself so much either."

Hannah blew a wild tendril of hair away from her face as though exasperated with his explanation. "Isn't it a little shallow to suddenly decide you don't love someone too?"

Rusty nodded and took some more popcorn, but he didn't eat it. He needed to make Hannah see just how sincere he was, because it seemed important.

"It's natural for a man to look at a woman, Hannah. It's also natural to admire her for her beauty. It's even natural for a man to want her. But that isn't very mature thinking. In fact, it isn't thinking at all. I guess since we've been wrangled into this marriage thing, I've given it more thought. Marriage was always a little elusive to me. When I looked at Jennifer today, I realized that her looks wouldn't carry over for years of marriage. Like...well...like the times in life when things don't go right. Would she stick around? I doubted it. And seriously, I felt I needed more. I needed someone I could talk to, someone I could rely on, someone I could worry and fret over. The minute she opened her mouth I knew she hadn't grown up one bit. She was still talking about her cheer-leading days, the prom, things that just don't matter any longer. She didn't need me any longer, maybe she never did. And maybe this is selfish Hannah, but a man likes to be needed."

Hannah sipped her hot chocolate and leaned back into the couch. She closed her eyes and Rusty stared long and hard at her. Hannah was such a mystery. He looked from the top of her wild head of dark hair to her legs that were tucked under her. He couldn't tell what she looked like under those clothes, but somehow it didn't seem important. He liked her just the way she was, he was comfortable with her, and tomorrow he was going to marry her! And somehow, that just didn't upset him any longer.

They watched I Love Lucy and when Rusty glanced over at her, she was sound asleep, with a soft little snore that tickled him.

He must be losing it, because that was one sexy little snore!

He stood up and waited to see if she would wake. When she didn't, he tucked the blanket around her and kissed her gently on the lips. Pepper raised his head, panted for a second then laid his head back down and whined a little.

"Night, Little darlin'."

She snored softly into his ear, and he smiled as he went to his bedroom.

# Chapter Nine

Hannah had slept all night on the couch. Strangely at peace. She woke up stiff and cranky the next morning though. She glanced about her to get her bearings. She rarely fell asleep on the couch, and when she did, it took a while to remember why. Pepper wasn't in sight. She somehow missed his friendly lick in the face.

She remembered the night all too well, and how she'd stared long and hard at Rusty as though she'd never seen a man in pajamas before.

After a quick shower, she went outside to tend to the stock. It was barely dawn and feeding the animals took priority over fixing breakfast. She'd made coffee and hurried out to the barn to finish up a few chores and feed the stock, but to her surprise Rusty had already taken care of most of it.

Without a word, she helped alongside him, as he tended them. The way they worked together, without the slightest disharmony scared her witless. She was too comfortable with him, she quickly decided. Occasionally she stole a glance in his direction, but he was paying her no mind and tending to business, like any other day. In silence they headed for the house together.

For a man about to get married, he seemed very calm, she thought. Unlike herself who was full of jitters and butterflies. This was a mistake, but there weren't many choices if she really wanted to save the ranch. If there had been any other way, she would have found it by now. She'd certainly agree to a quick divorce though, for his sake. He needed to know this, but from the look on his face she wasn't sure if this was the right time to talk about it.

As she made another pot of coffee an hour later, she listened as he talked about everything and anything but the wedding that was taking place in just a few short hours.

That made her nervous. How could he possibly be so calm? This wasn't some every day event.

When she finally sat down at the table with him and passed him the bacon and eggs, she approached the subject.

"How many people are coming?" She waited for him to answer impatiently.

He seemed to enjoy her discomfiture, if his lopsided grin was any measure.

"Oh, probably about fifty or so."

"Fifty?" she shouted and stood up. Had he lost his mind? Who in the world did he invite? The entire community? Was he crazy?

He grabbed her hand, unconsciously rubbing it in a circular motion, as though to calm her. "Sit down and eat your breakfast."

"But how could you invite so many people?" she began, the panic in her stomach unbearable. "The house...I need to clean."

"Sit down Hannah. The house is fine. And you'll be glad to know Jimmy's coming, too." His smile broadened.

With this news she stopped, looked at him, and her mouth flew open, but no words came out for a full minute.

He reached to close it, and she frowned. "How did you..."

"I simply invited him to the wedding."

"But...he couldn't just drop his business and come. He'd have to have notice."

"He had notice. I invited him last week. Besides, he told me he wouldn't miss your wedding for anything."

Hannah couldn't believe it. Rusty Travers had walked into her life and turned it upside down, again. She wasn't sure of anything anymore. She knew she should stop this whole thing, but how? With half the community arriving in a short time, she couldn't do a thing.

"How could you have known we would be married, a week ago?"

"I said we were getting married this weekend, I meant it. The fifteenth is next Friday. I plan to have that loan by then."

She dropped her fork and pushed her plate away. For some reason connecting the loan and the wedding together in the same sentence irritated her.

"You better eat, little darlin'."

"I can't. My insides are jumping out at me." she said then looked up at him with a startled expression. "I mean...getting married. We're really going to...get married?"

"Yes ma'am." He grinned, took his hat off and dug into the bacon and eggs with vigor as though the subject was closed, and he was satisfied.

"Aren't you even the least bit nervous?" She asked taking a big swig of coffee that she quickly spewed in the opposite direction. Rusty came to her side, patted her on the back and offered her an amused smile.

"I thought I'd be. I really did, but I'm not. Yes, it's a wedding, but it won't change a whole lot. Especially since you set the terms for the marriage. The only thing that's gonna change is your credit, and your marital status." He sat down, took another bite and watched her closely.

"You can still back out you know..."she offered him the out.

"No ma'am, I can't." The smile faded from his handsome lips but remained in his eyes.

"Why not?" she questioned her voice rising with her irritation.

"I gave you my word on it. I'm a Travers, and the Travers give their word, they keep it, for one thing. For another, I like you Hannah...and that's the first step."

Hannah's gaze turned on him like cold ice water. "First step to what?"

"To a marriage. You should like someone before you marry them, don't you think?"

Hannah moistened her bottom lip and looked away. She got to her feet. Yes, she agreed with him and yes, she liked him too, but this wasn't to be a real marriage. Keeping that upper-most in her mind kept her sane. "The sooner we get this over with, the better..."

"Anxious, Darlin'?" His devilish grin made her nervous.

"No, I'm terrified." He could take this with a grain of salt, but taking vows, in front of witnesses made her full of uncertainties. "And would you please quit calling me...that!"

"You don't like Darlin'?" His head twisted to one side as he smiled. "Honey, sweetie, sugar cakes...?" He teased with a light in those ultra-blue eyes. "Oh, come on Hannah. Have a heart will ya? I'm not a beast," he said and covered her hand with his own.

She jerked free and stood up. "I'm going to take a bath."

"Hmm....like baths better than showers?"

Hannah looked perplexed again. "Never thought about it, but yes, I guess I do. After sitting the saddle most of the day, a good warm bath is just the trick to relax me." But the mere mention of sitting a saddle had her thinking about the moment they shared at the 4 Bar None. The moment she realized she wanted more of Rusty Travers.

"A bath can be quite pleasurable...especially with the right company." He grinned.

Now she was fuming, and he had to admit, she looked gorgeous when she blushed. He hated to tease her so, but it was fun, and it was his wedding day. A man should have fun on his wedding day he reasoned. This would be about all he'd get, he reckoned.

*****

Hannah ran the water for her bath, adding her usual fragrance to the water and testing the temperature. All her actions seemed normal, except the slight shake to her hands, the little furrows on her brow and the tension in her entire body.

Could she actually do this?

Why was he so intent on doing this? And acting as though he actually looked forward to it! She didn't understand him. She didn't want pretenses either. He should be angry, upset, and not at all willing. That she could understand. And she should be mad at him, but for the life of her, all she could think of was how wonderful he was being. She didn't want him being wonderful. She wished he was irritable like her.

She stepped into the full tub of water and surrounded herself with the silk of the warm water, trying to relax. It seemed impossible when she suddenly realized that this man, this Rusty Travers was going to be her husband in a few short hours. The real scare was how she'd keep her hands to herself, afterwards. Should she bar the door to her bedroom? Would he insist? They hadn't even discussed that!

Husband!

She closed her eyes and immediately the picture of him standing in her hall doorway in those red checked pajamas and cowboy hat was priceless. She had gawked at him like a schoolgirl. But it wasn't all her fault. He was magnificent. She had committed unknowingly to memory every inch of him. Her body had responded to him unwillingly, she told herself.

Maybe she could lie to herself about staring at him, but that night on the horse, she had wanted him in no uncertain terms, and if she read him right, he wanted her too. Even though that was merely a physical wanting, it was so intense, so needy, she couldn't put it out of her mind.

She could almost picture him standing at the door now, looking in. With that big brown cowboy hat on, and little else.

Keeping her hands off her new husband would be the greatest challenge she had ever faced, but for both their sakes she had to do it. She wouldn't allow him to ruin his life over her problems and she couldn't allow herself to completely fall in love with the man. Could she?

No, she couldn't. This marriage wasn't based on love, she had to remember that.

She opened her eyes and continued to bathe. But as she touched herself, she felt the heat radiate through her, and for just a moment, she imagined them coming together. That was pure imagination, nothing more, she assured herself, and it would never happen again. She wouldn't let it.

*****

A couple of hours later Hannah found herself standing in her living room greeting guests, all fifty some odd of them.

Josey hurriedly whisked her away by telling her it was bad luck to see the groom before marriage. Hannah protested that the preacher was arriving, and she should be there to greet him, but Josey shook her head.

"I don't think he'll expect it, today, Miss Hannah, now come on. We've got to get you ready."

Hannah obeyed her but put little stock in old sayings about brides. Josey seemed to know all about weddings and such. She insisted Hannah should wear baby's breath in her hair to go with the beautiful red rose bouquet sprinkled with baby's breath that Rusty had sent to her from the florist shop in town. How had Rusty found so much time to take care of so many details? Most men wouldn't even think of such things.

He must have called them too, on his cell phone, she reflected as she stared at the bouquet. It was hard not to love the beautiful red roses peeking through the tissue paper at her.

Hannah fingered the roses. Flowers were a weakness, she thought, but one she wanted to indulge in today. After all, she certainly didn't plan on having another wedding in her lifetime. And all her dreams of marrying the right man, for the right reasons came front and center and made her wish it might be real.

She glanced in the mirror as she pulled out her mother's wedding dress. It had already been to the cleaners thanks to Josey, and Hannah hesitated to take it out of the bag. Josey gasped.

"It is beautiful, Miss Hannah."

"I don't even know if it still fits," Hannah cried, as a tear escaped down her cheek. She remembered trying it on long ago, on her first visit home from Las Vegas. When she thought Vic loved her and was about to propose to her. Wild dreams. Vic never cared, she nearly laughed now at her folly. That had been nothing more than a giant crush on her handsome boss. It didn't compare to the feelings she had for Rusty. Dear God, she was in love with Rusty. How could she have let herself in for such a big fall? Hadn't she learned anything from her experiences?

But that stopped her cold for a minute. Wait! She couldn't have feelings for Rusty. Nothing more than friendship. Keeping him at arm's distance was best, no matter what. Because if Vic had hurt her, she could imagine what losing Rusty would do to her heart. She had to keep herself at a distance.

Yes, distance was the answer!

Slowly she peeled her clothes from her body and stepped into the dress. Josey gasped again and cried, throwing her hands in the air with such dramatic flair, Hannah thought she was sick.

"You are so beautiful. Why do you hide behind those ugly clothes? Don't you want a man to love you?" Josey insisted scowling as she helped to zip the dress.

"Didn't want anyone getting any ideas. Besides, when the right man comes along, he'll love me despite the clothes, and I'll know it's the real thing. I want a man to love me...not my body."

"Maybe, but you can't hide beauty, honey. And I think your Mr. Rusty sees right through your disguise. I've seen the way he looks at you." Josey hugged her then moved away and wiped the tears from her eyes. "I'm so happy for you."

Hannah opened her mouth to stay Josey's emotions, but then thought better of it. No use ruining Josey's dreams. From the time she was a small girl Josey had mothered Hannah and they had become family. Josey was as close to a mother as Hannah was gonna have and ruining this day for her would hurt her. She'd be quiet.

But when she zipped the dress, Hannah fit right into it, as though it had been made for her. Even Hannah couldn't believe it. She wondered wildly if she was being a bit too presumptuous about wearing this dress. Perhaps she should have stuck with the one she originally bought for the occasion. A plain white A-line dress, with no frills. Still, Rusty had gone to a lot of expense to prove a point, and this wedding dress would help drive home the fact that they were really getting married. Going through all the motions...and emotions. Business or not, it was still a marriage and in the sight of God, she reminded herself. Could she possibly take such a vow and not mean it?

She glanced in the mirror and her eyes became big, pools of tears. Seeing herself as a bride shocked her into reality. Dear God, she was about to marry Rusty Travers!

The bodice was fitted, and her small but perfect breasts pouted pleasingly against the top of her gown. The long white puffy satin sleeves were adorned with pearls and lace. The skirt was long and full, and the train dragged a good yard or two.

A knock came at the door, and Josey went to answer it. Jimmy came in.

"My God, Hannah, you're beautiful honey!" He cried lifting her into his arms and twirling her about.

Hannah laughed and cried and hugged her brother with all her might.

"I'm so scared." She admitted her knees knocking like two drums against each other.

"Hey, he's a pretty nice fella. I just met him. He's sure acting proud as a peacock." Jimmy smiled at her as he set her down and eyed her again.

"You look like Mama." He said, his voice going low.

"I can barely remember her," she cried.

"Yeah, me too. If it weren't for all the pictures I probably wouldn't." Jimmy shrugged. "You've got to meet my wife. I'll call her in, if you don't mind."

Hannah wished she had a few more minutes alone with him, but he seemed bent on making introductions. Hannah felt awkward shaking hands with the beautiful blonde that waltzed elegantly into the bedroom.

Pam wasted no time in hugging her, "I'm so very happy to meet you Hannah. Jimmy's told me so much about you. I feel I know you."

Hannah smiled. She knew nothing of her except what Jimmy had managed to write in his letters. They were strangers, but the smile on her face told Hannah they would soon be friends.

Josey was introduced to Pam when she came back in with the long flowing veil and after a lot of making over her dress and the wedding arrangements, Hannah was finally alone in the room.

She glanced at the bed. Her bed. Would Rusty expect her to share it? It wasn't part of the bargain and she couldn't think about that now. The wedding march was playing, and Jimmy knocked to take her arm and guide her down the narrow little pathway of her living room to where her handsome husband-to-be stood staring. He looked at her from head to foot and smiled as he took her arm from Jimmy.

Hannah couldn't take her eyes off Rusty. He was so virile and handsome today she lost her breath several times. Was she breathing? She doubted it.

Rusty was wearing a dark blue western suit, and bolero tie against a light blue silk shirt. He had a silver Stetson on and his boots were shined. The way his muscles stretched against his jacket when he moved, made Hannah twice as aware of him as she should be. She found herself looking at him closely and liking the way his mouth twitched just a bit as he looked at her. She saw something in his expression that told her he was fulfilling his promise to her, and maybe more. Her heart leapt.

Hannah felt light headed, as though she weren't really here. As though all these people were watching her get married, thinking it was for real. There was a sea of faces behind her, but she didn't see any of them because quite frankly she couldn't take her eyes off Rusty.

The ceremony was over before she realized it, and the preacher was smiling and saying," You can kiss the bride now..."

Rusty turned to her, smiled devilishly down into her surprised face and took her mouth in a hot kiss that melted her bones, and had their audience sighing with pleasure. Her knees buckled for a fraction as his tongue slid warmly into her mouth and caressed hers. He seemed intent on relishing the moment, but even then, he was holding her up, determined to get her through this moment of bliss without marring the perfect ceremony.

When he finally let her go, she heard the slightest groan, but couldn't decide whether it came from him, or herself. She turned away, to hide the desire on her face and smiled at the congregation that was now hovering around them.

"Okay, leave a little for the rest of us Rusty," Deke chuckled as he took Hannah into his arms and kissed her lightly on the lips. Then Clint and Jake had a turn with her. Jimmy came to stand by her side. He kissed her and smiled into her worried eyes.

"You okay, sis?"

"Yes, of course," she managed brightly, hoping no one heard her knees knocking.

Rusty was by her side, holding her elbow, even it shivered. She was grateful for once to be held up, for she wasn't sure she could manage it. God, how could she keep her nerves from falling apart?

All her school friends stood waiting to tell her how beautiful she looked, her ranch hands looked a little stunned as they'd never seen the boss dressed like this.

One by one, they kissed her cheek and congratulated Rusty.

Then Burt walked up to her, his face serene, he shook Rusty's hand and looked into her eyes, "Be good to her."

"I intend to." Rusty answered meeting the warning with a smile.

Burt leaned over to kiss her cheek, and whispered, "If you ever need me..."

Hannah looked from one to the other, and then Rusty whispered as Burt turned and walked away. "I invited him. I thought it only right."

Hannah nodded her approval.

Why was Rusty doing this? Why did he insist on all these people, all this expense? The flowers, she hadn't expected, all over her living room only minutes before the wedding. The actual wedding ring that matched the engagement ring...the one Jennifer should be wearing she reminded herself, trying to bring some level of sanity to the day.

Minutes later they cut the cake and he shoved a small piece in her mouth as a photographer captured the moment. Photographer? Where had he come from, she wondered? But it was the way he shoved it into her mouth, almost erotic in motion. No... she was over-reacting. He wasn't thinking those things. Was he?

"You've got one fine young man there Hannah. Be gentle with him."

Hannah wondered at Emma's words, but there was little time to ponder as a fiddler struck up the music and the dancing began.

Hannah met Clint and Abby, and Jake had come all the way from Peaceful for the event. There was no problem in keeping the names straight though, each Travers brother had a completely different personality.

Jimmy walked up to Rusty and shook his hand solemnly; he glanced at her and whispered, "We'll talk later, hon."

Then Rusty walked off with him for a few minutes.

Hannah wondered what Jimmy was saying to her new husband. She hoped he wouldn't talk about her job in Vegas. She wanted to do that personally, if the time ever came for it.

Jimmy had made no bones about the fact that he hated what his sister had done for a living but agreed it did put him through school and that it wouldn't be a topic for discussion. She only hoped he remembered that now.

She secretly wished she had more time to visit with Jimmy, but knew it wasn't the best time to seek him out. It had been a long time and there was so much catching up she wanted to do.

When a slow waltz filtered through the full living room, Rusty looked for Hannah in the crowd of people. It didn't take him long to spot her, she noticed. Then he took her into his arms. Hannah laughed and pretended a lightheartedness she wasn't feeling. Yet being in Rusty's arms again immediately brought the sexual tension front and center and Hannah struggled to remember that this wasn't for real and that Rusty didn't really love her.

Funny how that thought kept bouncing around in her head.

Mr. Simmons talked with Rusty for a few minutes afterwards and Hannah wanted desperately to know what he might have said, but there wasn't a time to ask. Maybe later, she told herself as she turned a smile on her guests and tried to keep focused.

Rusty showered her with attention and was quite the gentleman, kissing her on the cheek endlessly, nibbling on her neck and smiling as though he were the happiest man alive. Hannah tried to match him, but the quiver in her knees threatened to send her to the floor several times.

Altogether it was a day Hannah was ready to end. The tension between her and Rusty seemed electrical at moments and she had the greatest tendency to run. Her heart was at stake and somehow, she had to remember this wasn't for real.

Then Deke got everyone's attention, by clanging his champagne glass with a spoon.

"It's pretty traditional in this family to have a honeymoon. And Rusty and Hannah are gonna have a great one. Me, Clint and Jake are seeing to that. We've arranged for a surprise honeymoon for the two of them. Their Lear-jet is waiting so we need to wrap things up here. While Hannah changes, we'll make arrangements to get as many to the airport as possible."

Hannah's eyes got big and she cut a glance at Rusty. Without a word, he gathered her in his arms, and brought her close, "Play along with this. If Simmons had any doubts as to my collateral, it will be gone now." Rusty whispered and then kissed her.

It was meant to be a small kiss of affection, but all the excitement keying the air at the moment as some wanted to ride to the small air strip to see them off and Hannah found herself drowning in the kiss. As though hanging on to her new husband was the last remnant of sanity left. He tasted so good, smelled so divine.

When they broke apart, Clint raised a whoop and several hats were tossed in the air.

He released her to Josey who whisked her off to the bedroom again to change. Hannah hurried, her mind a blur of the events. Now what? A honeymoon was the last thing she expected. Her nerves were a frazzle. How could she cope with this added pressure?

But as she joined Rusty again, she didn't see one sign of hesitation with him. In fact, he seemed almost eager.

Hannah stood frozen to the spot, until Rusty picked her up in his arms and carried her to the limo awaiting them outside.

# Chapter Ten

The minute Rusty got behind the wheel of the jet, Hannah shut the cabin door and joined him in the other seat. She was full of questions, but her stomach churned for a few moments. Being in the plane made her queasiness return and she sat quietly for a while, trying to keep her stomach in control.

"H-how did..."

Rusty was busy with the instrument panel for several minutes and finally when airborne he turned to her, knowing she was full of questions.

"Calm down, Hannah. It's all just to impress your Mr. Simmons. And I'd say from his sheepish expression when he saw the Lear-jet, he was mighty impressed."

"Is it...yours?"

"No," Rusty answered checking yet another switch. "I've been taking flying lessons from a buddy of mine. It's a loan."

She nodded woodenly. "Well...that explains that, then, but..."

"No self-respecting groom would marry a beautiful woman and not take her on a honeymoon, now would they? Simmons would expect it. We had to come up with something."

"I see, so where are we going?"

"To Vegas!"

"Vegas...?" Her heart did a flip-flop and her stomach did a dive. Vegas! "But...the ranch.... I can't just leave."

"It's all taken care of. Deke's letting several of our hands stay on the place until we get back."

Hannah slumped into the seat and laid her head back, so she could rest it. She was tired, mainly from all the keyed-up tension that had surrounded the entire ceremony, and now this, so unexpected. And Vegas!

"Don't fret Little Darlin'. This isn't costing us much, none of it."

"What about the limo?" Hannah protested.

"Deke took care of that. I don't know if he paid for it, or what. Knowing Deke, it was probably just a return favor from a friend. You'll have to ask him."

Hannah shook her head in amazement. "Well, I have to hand it to you, when you set out to impress, you do a bang-up job, Mr. Travers."

"Thanks, Mrs. Travers."

Mrs. Travers? The fact that she'd just married this man, legally, hit her again. Also, the fact that he had done everything in his power to impress the banker, make sure he was at the wedding, and all her friends too, made her confident now that they would get the loan without a problem. The ranch was saved!

Elated and fearful of this trip, she gripped her chair arms. She should have told Rusty all about her job in Vegas, and then she wouldn't be facing it now. But how? What would he think of her? She'd have to wait until the right time came. And hope she didn't run into anyone she knew before that time came.

They landed on a small private strip just the other side of North Las Vegas and rented a car to drive to the hotel.

Hannah had an awful feeling that this trip would soon catch up with her, but there was little she could do. Until she could figure out how to break it to him, she had to trust her instincts to guide her. Surely, he would understand.

But now they were truly alone. And that fact hit Hannah like a tidal wave. What was she going to do with her handsome husband now?

What did Rusty have in mind?

Rusty seemed unaware of her qualms as he escorted her into the lobby of Caesar's Palace. She felt the blood leave her face, as she walked up to the desk. Would anyone working here recognize her? Just down the street was

Bally's and the Indigo Lounge where she'd worked. Had it only been a few months before that she'd been one of the line-ups for the Jubilee Theater? As long as she didn't run into Vic, she might be alright. At least until she found a way to tell Rusty about her life here.

Rusty not only took the keys to their room but signed them up for a tour of the Hoover Dam, a show, and took a brochure on the sites about town. He handed the brochures to her as he took her elbow and they followed the bellman to their room.

"You've picked a Spa Deluxe Room, one of our finest," the bellman said with a smile as he motioned for Hannah to enter the room.

Hannah was immediately immersed in fascinating decorum of golds and ambers. The frosted glass windows that separated the huge bath from the double beds in the main room distracted while Rusty tipped the bellman.

"This is beautiful," she sighed as she sank herself into one of the big double beds and rolled on it.

"I'm glad you approve." Rusty chuckled.

"It looks terribly expensive though, Rusty." Hannah said thinking about the expense of it all.

"This room was reasonable, considering others, and for what we get. But don't get too comfortable. We'll dine at Terrazza's tonight, since it's in the hotel. They have fantastic rack of lamb. Then tomorrow we'll do a tour, see a show, and maybe even gamble a little." He teased with a gentle tugging of her arm. "So, change clothes if you wish, casual to dressy, and let's get a bite to eat before we call it a night. I'd like to walk down to the Bellagio and show you a beautiful display of water and lights tonight. You'll love it."

Hannah realized the depth of his intentions to show her a good time and she was overwhelmed.

Before she could object to his expenditures, he was shooing her into the luxurious bath and she was stunned at the magnificent marble counters and tiles. She felt like a Roman princess tonight. Could she possibly be dreaming?

By the pool an hour or so later, she watched the shimmering water play its magic on her heart. If this were a real honeymoon, she'd be so speechless. The succulent rack of lamb was dusted with pecorinos Romano cheese. It tempted and delighted her taste buds. She totally approved of Rusty's choice.

Even later they walked to the Bellagio and watched along the walkway as the water and the beautiful colors and music brought it all to life.

Hannah had lived here for nearly three years and not once had she enjoyed the luxuries that Rusty was allowing her. She'd dreamed of staying at Caesar's Palace, at dining at an elegant restaurant, at taking the time to enjoy the sites of this magnificent tinsel town. But during that time, she had worked her butt off to support her brother and father and hadn't had those luxuries. Now he was making her dreams come true. Offering her another world to discover.

As they slowly made their way back to the hotel, Hannah realized that Bally's was in between the two hotels. She held her breath as she passed the familiarly lit Bally's.

She had to tell Rusty about her dancing. Hannah refrained from going to the bed again, instead she sat on the floor, watching TV for a while, and then glanced at Rusty several times. What handsome man she had married, too handsome. He still wore his western tux, and she had changed into a silk pantsuit, but looked dressy, Josey had told her.

Rusty ordered wine from room service and settled next to her on the floor

"I didn't even ask if you liked wine?" He asked as he tried to put her at ease.

"It's just what I needed." She laughed, all the tension drained and replaced by a warm fuzzy feeling as she sipped the fruity wine. She wasn't used to wine, but she knew enough not to gulp it down.

"Tomorrow we'll take the tour, how's that?" Rusty suggested as he took the last sip of his wine and then took her glass and set it aside.

They were watching Ghost.

Hannah smiled and turned to look at him with tears in her eyes. "That sounds like fun. But I really feel guilty up here enjoying myself while Deke's men take care of things."

"Consider yourself on vacation. You like this movie?"

"I love it. I always thought it portrayed death well, and the hereafter. I'd like to think that is what it will be like. You know...the white light coming to get you."

"Or the dark?"

"Or the dark." she giggled.

"I like it too. I especially like the fact that he takes care of her, even in death, as a ghost. A man should see to his woman."

"Yeah," she choked a little and turned so he couldn't see her face.

Rusty took her hands and pulled her down on the furry rug on the floor so they could both prop up against the foot of the bed.

It was deliriously warm, and Hannah was too tired to argue. She didn't snuggle against him, although the thought occurred to her. Instead she tried to concentrate on the flickering movie. In any other instance this might be romantic, but she fully realized she had to keep her head. After all, it wasn't a real honeymoon.

"So, what do you think of Las Vegas?"

"It's fabulous." It was a lead for her to tell him about her life here, but somehow, she couldn't quite break the spell he was weaving for them. "This hotel is an absolute dream...."

She tried to concentrate strictly on the movie but Rusty was nipping at her cheek and the warmth that suddenly surrounded them enveloped them in a cocoon of their own. Her breathing seemed nonexistent, as his kisses brought all her attention to his desire ridden face.

She squirmed when his lips nibbled at her ear. She wanted him, he wanted her, so why couldn't it be, she asked herself. Because this is a dream, silly!

"I'm not gonna hurt you Hannah," he whispered hoarsely.

"I know…but this is a little too cozy," she said and forced herself up and away from his tempting arms. "Rusty, I appreciate what you are doing for me, but I'm not forgetting our bargain."

"Bargain?"

"This isn't a real marriage...and I'm sure you won't forget that."

"Not as long as you keep reminding me...." he didn't look at her but stared off into the distance.

Rusty frowned but he didn't argue the point. Guilt made her more amendable.

"Yeah," he moved to get up and gathered his coat. From the quick movements and the exaggerated way, he struggled into his coat, she could tell he wasn't happy with her. But what did he expect? "I guess I better go downstairs for a while. Let you get ready for bed."

"That's a good idea," she breathed a sigh. Still, the room went cold when he walked out. Hannah shivered. She really enjoyed snuggling with him, and a small part of her wished it could last, but she was too sensible for that.

He stared at her over his shoulder at the door until she was forced to look straight at him. Something in his expression nearly made her weaken and go to him, but she made herself stay where she was. It was just too tempting. It would only lead to heartbreak later, her good sense reminded her.

"I think I'll take a quick shower and get ready for bed. Which bed do you want?" She asked not daring to look at him now.

"Doesn't matter," he said with obvious exasperation. Then he was gone, leaving behind the cold breeze that crept from the doorway. It wasn't the wind that was cold. It was her. But how was she supposed to treat her husband? Her husband! Would she ever get used to those words?

What had he expected? She wasn't about to play bedroom pals with him now. Just because they were married didn't mean she was changing a thing. Except those kisses by the fire stirred much more than her imagination, and she was feeling as exasperated as he. So much so, she was on edge.

Shrugging off the desire of her own body, she headed for the small bathroom. A good warm shower, and sleep would shake off this feeling of need within her.

*****

Unable to keep himself busy any longer, Rusty came back. He checked the doors and the beds for the long night ahead of him. He was about to check on the blankets when he passed the bathroom and saw it was cracked open. It suddenly dawned on him that he hadn't checked to see if there were towels or soap or anything. He peeked through the doorway. Good, she was still in the shower, he couldn't really see her, just a vague outline, so he tiptoed in to get the towels out of the cabinet and lay them on the top of the commode. He was about to set them down and leave when she opened the curtain and gasped.

"Oh-uh..." his jaw dropped, his breath left his lungs, and he stood there, the towel slipping from his fingers as he stared at his wife. All of his wife.

She was beautiful! And every nerve in his body sprang to alertness as his gaze took her in slowly. He couldn't move, couldn't think for an instant. His body was sending out signals to his brain, but he refused to listen. Hannah had been hiding, but why? He had known she was hiding, but he figured she hid her imperfections from him, not her beauty.

Instinct had him grabbing the towel and slowly handing it to her as she stepped toward it. Her eyes were as big as saucers, and they connected to his. Minutes seemed to pass, but it was only seconds.

They both seemed speechless at the moment.

Then Rusty rushed to explain..."I'm sorry. I thought you'd need this." His voice was low, throaty.

He took the towel and gently wrapped it around her small but perfect body. As his fingers brushed the cleavage of her breasts he frowned down into her face. Tension electrified the air. He was mere inches from her. Steam from her shower wafted between them. Desire loomed like a fragile thread. Had the lights flickered, a match lit, or just the flames from his expression warmed her face.

Everything inside Rusty ignited into an inferno of desire, but he intentionally squashed it, knowing full well, that acting on his own needs would not win Hannah's favor. He had to win her heart. And he wanted her heart.

"Any more surprises Hannah?" he asked his voice low and husky.

"Surprises?" Her voice was faint, breathless.

"Baggy pants, big shirts, floppy hat. Ugly clothes, to detract any man. So, what are you hiding from?" His face was a mass of conflicting emotions.

"N-nothing," she held the towel as though it were her lifeline. But he saw the quiver in her fingers, on her lips.

"Or who?" he said as though it were something bad. "There's got to be an explanation Hannah. Can't you tell me?"

"Rusty, please."

"Were you hiding from me?"

"No," she reacted too quickly, her eyes flashing with something he didn't recognize.

And then he did. Hannah was afraid of love...and somehow, he had to teach her that love could be the most wonderful thing in the world. If what he felt for Hannah was even half of what his father felt for his mother, then he was on the right track at last. But how would he ever convince her now, that he loved her for herself, not her beauty.

"You're beautiful Hannah." He rasped.

She gazed at him in shock. "Please don't flatter me..."

His eyes warmed her. "This might surprise you, Hannah, but I've always found you enchanting. You charmed me with your cuteness a long time ago. I've been intrigued with you from the beginning, not able to put my finger on what makes my feelings for you grow. I liked you. Hannah, and not because of what you looked like, but rather in spite of it. There was something about you Hannah. I thought there was something special about you before I ever saw your body. And now that I have, it makes no difference at all. And I know that sounds pretty damned crazy coming from me."

The smile didn't quite reach her lips. "I'm very tired, could we talk about this in the morning?" she moved to go past him.

"No, I think we should talk about it now. What's going on here?  Why the masquerade?"

She leaned against the doorframe. "You wouldn't understand."

"Try me."

She paused and stared at him. The old feelings came rushing to the front. "I don't want to be pawed and manhandled. If I want a man, I'll do the choosing."

"That's fair enough, but can't you just tell a man?" He asked his spirits lifting for a moment.

"You wouldn't understand it."

"Give me a little credit, Hannah."

"I can't talk about this now, please." she cried and ran for the bed nearest the bathroom.

He walked out of the bathroom slowly. He wondered how he had done such a thing. Never had he felt so right about wanting a woman. He also knew Hannah wasn't completely immune to him either. And damn she was beautiful. This only complicated things, though. He knew she was cute, he'd fallen for that cuteness. Those baggy clothes only made him more curious as to what she was hiding. But this! What was she hiding?

He hadn't touched her. Wouldn't touch her. He couldn't. If Hannah had taught him anything, it was that love wasn't physical. He knew if he went after her now, she'd think that. Especially after he made over Jennifer so. He reviled himself for talking on and on about how gorgeous Jennifer was around Hannah. How shallow he had been. And Hannah had witnessed it.

So how could he make her understand what he was feeling? How could he let Hannah know he was falling in love with her? Her! Not the package, although she certainly had one beautiful package he itched to hold again.

Oh, he knew what he was feeling alright. White-hot desire...that's what. Right this minute, he wanted her so bad he wouldn't sleep most the night because of it. But he also knew that wouldn't work with Hannah. He wasn't just going to work his way into her bed. Somehow, he had to work himself into her heart, first. He had to convince her of the rightness of it. That she was different. Now that he knew what love was about, he had to convince her he knew. He suddenly realized she had torn down a wall and erected a bigger one.

Why would any woman hide such a beautiful body? Not that he expected her to parade around like a common...no, not Hannah.

Had someone hurt her? She'd do the picking she said. Now that was an outstanding thought. Only problem was...how was she going to pick him?

He would have to think this out, and he hoped it kept him up all night thinking, because what he wanted to do was make her his woman, tonight.

This was a totally new experience for him. He was in love with Hannah. And not just because he suddenly found her beautiful. He had liked her before he ever saw her body. He had liked kissing her. But so far, he'd only managed to convince her he wanted her. And knowing Hannah like he did, that wouldn't be enough.

He took the other bed. He tried to go to sleep, but her milling around in the bathroom minutes later had him curious as to what she wore to bed.

Damn! White silk. White silk is what she wore to bed, and lovely as a picture. And her hair, that wild head of dark hair that seemed to know no real direction cascaded over her shoulders like a dark cloud. Then he smiled to himself and licked his lips, yes, like a dark cloud of heavenly chocolate. His fingers itched to run through it.

He gathered his blankets and jumped into the cold bed he'd made wrestling with the pillow for what seemed like hours.

This was the longest night of his life. And the most miserable...

"Goodnight," she called from the other bed.

"Goodnight," he wailed miserably not far away.

*****

But the night wore slowly on and all the tossing and turning didn't help.

"Hannah, you asleep?" he called to her from the darkness.

"No... why?" she asked quietly.

"You as miserable as I am?" He asked.

"Miserable?"

"Let's don't play games, Hannah. We want each other...plain and simple."

He heard her voice hitch, in a short gasp. He'd shocked her.

"I'm not having sex with you Rusty, I'm sorry. I thought you understood the terms of this marriage." She protested weakly.

"Terms? I didn't know there were any terms. Good thing you told me." He quipped hitting the pillow and glancing through the darkness for her.

"I wasn't thinking of having sex, Hannah. I was...thinking—about making love." He sighed heavily as though the subject were closed. "There's a difference you know."

"I know...I mean..." Hannah's voice drifted away.

"Well...what's so bad about making love Hannah? You want it as much as I do...I saw it in your eyes today." He muttered miserably.

"Maybe...for a moment. I'm sorry Rusty. I'm not that sophisticated. I haven't...I mean...I never..."

"Oh God, tell me it isn't true..." Rusty sat up straight in bed and stared at the darkness.

"What?" she sat up in the other bed expectantly.

"Tell me you aren't a virgin." He moaned biting the pillow and spitting it out.

"That's none of your business." she said miserably, drowning her voice and tears into her pillow.

"You are, aren't you?" He whispered, and suddenly he was standing by her bed.

She pulled the sheet up over her and covered her head and all. "And what if I am?" she mumbled through the sheet.

He chuckled.

"Do you have to laugh at me, like that."

"I'm not laughing at you, honey. I'm laughing with you."

"No, I'm kind of a one-woman man, Hannah."

"Oh."

She felt the mattress give as his knee moved toward her. "The first time should be special Hannah. With someone who cares about you."

"I know that," she cried out, as the bed began to shake with her fear.

"I care Hannah...." He reached through the darkness for her, and then moved away, off the bed. "That's why I'm not going to touch you...until you are ready."

It was a whisper in the night, but she heard it and uncovered her head just a little.

"Thank you," she managed, and felt the tears falling as she heard him returning to his own bed. "Rusty..." she called out to him

He hesitated but didn't look over his shoulder at her.

"His name was Vic Trusdale. I thought I loved him. He's the one that hurt me."

This sudden admission had Rusty more than pausing. He turned around and stared through the darkness at her then he came and sat on the edge of the bed, looking down at her and wondering just how much this Vic Trusdale had hurt her. He wanted to hurt the man. For hurting Hannah.

"Did he...?"

"No," she rushed to answer. "We never did. Although, I was almost ready to give in to him until I found him with another woman. A co-worker. He was the first man I ever cared about. I thought he cared too. He didn't. At least not that way. I was naive, young, silly even."

Rusty hung his head. All of this news had startled him, but he knew he had taken a giant step with Hannah tonight, even though they hadn't made love. Hannah was learning to trust him. And that was a start. He smiled sadly at her, put his hand on her arm and nodded, "Thanks for telling me about it."

"Goodnight, and thanks for listening."

"Anytime, little darlin'."

Now he could sleep!

Or could he? Hannah had just shared something important with him. Was it his turn?

"Hannah," he called softly through the darkness.

"Yes," Hannah raised up in the bed.

"It's my turn to confess something..." He said lowly. "I really wasn't laughing at you."

"It's alright." Hannah seemed to hold her breath, as though waiting.

"I've never confessed this to anyone. But, I've never." his voice drifted off into space. "Either."

"You haven't?" Hannah rushed to ask.

"No. Jennifer and I agreed early on, not to. We had this notion that it would be something to look forward too, later. Anyway, we never."

"Is she the only girl you ever went with?"

"Yeah, I'm afraid I'm a one-woman kind of guy."

There was a long silence, he could almost hear her breathing. He wished he could rush into her bed, take her in his arms and hold her, but he knew he'd frighten her. He wanted to be gentle with Hannah.

"Hannah...have you...ever imagined what it might be like?" Rusty asked as he pushed himself down into the softness of the bed.

He heard her voice catch as she spoke. "Sometimes."

"Would you mind if I share what I think it *should* be like?" He asked, almost turning to stare into the darkness at her.

The gasp told him, she was holding her breath for his words. He smiled to himself.

He laid back, threw his arms over his head and closed his eyes.

"When a man and a woman come together..." he began slowly, his voice softening as he imagined it in his mind. "Well...it should mean something. It should mean they are committed to each other...in every way. Don't you agree?"

"Y-yes," she laid down too. He wondered if she closed her eyes and if she was imagining it too.

"Okay, this is what I would do...Hannah...if I was in love with a woman." He clarified that, so she would know this wasn't just some sexual arousal.

"We'd have dated a while, got to know each other well. Only not too well. I think knowing a woman too well can complicate it all. But anyway, when I decided she was right for me, and I was right for her...that's when it would happen."

The silence from the other bed made him nervous, but he felt he had to share this with her. "We'd have a nice quiet dinner, I'd give her a rose, just a single rose, I think. Mainly because to appreciate something as beautiful as a rose, it should be separate from others. Special sort of. We'd gaze into each other's eyes, and I'd know she loved me, just from the look in those eyes. We'd be sitting on the couch, probably. I'd put my arm around her, until she was really comfortable with it. Then I'd lean over and kiss her, real gentle like. If she kissed me back, I'd let her know how much I wanted her by my movements, and my kisses. I pick her up and carry her to my bed, kicking the door closed, so no one would disturb us. I'd lay her down on the bed and smother her with kisses until I knew she was wanting more. And I'd know too, by the look in her eyes, and the way she breathed. I'd want to kiss every part of her, slowly, enjoying every inch of her. I'd like to see her body, and watch it react to my kisses too."

"H-how do you know it would react to you...?"

"I don't for sure. But I know mine does...so hers would too."

He sat up, shaking himself a little. This was getting him nowhere, but he had to go on. He had to tell her how it would be.

"I wouldn't rush her. But if she responded, I'd slowly begin to peel away her clothes, toss them on the floor, and let her do the same with me. She'd be beautiful to me, even if she had a pot belly, and a mustache under her nose. You see, I kind of imagined you might have a pot belly you were hiding under those clothes. I never once thought you were hiding your beauty. Anyway, they say love is blind, and I'm inclined to agree. I'd be kissing her all the time we were doing this, so as to build the fire between us. And I think as I kissed her, I'd tell her what I thought of each and every part of her. Starting with who she was...what she was...and what she could become. I'd touch and kiss her breasts with a reverence because to me, it's that exact body part that makes her a woman, different from me. I'd take some time to explore, both the tips and beneath. You have lovely breasts, by the way." His breath caught as though he were experiencing it right now.

There was a silence from the other bed.

"I'd not only let her but want her to touch me all over too. I'd tell her what pleased me. Just like I hope she'd tell me. Because when a man and a woman come together for the first time, they need to talk about it, understand it, enjoy it. My hands," he took his hands out of the blanket and looked at them. "My hands would probably tremble as they found there way downward... First time and all. I know what to expect, I've seen pictures," He chuckled softly.

He stared at his hands, they were trembling, as though he were visibly touching Hannah now. A cool sweat broke over him as he continued to explain his feelings. Every part of him stirred to life at his own words. When he closed his eyes, he could almost feel Hannah beneath him. Still he continued.

"Where my hands went, my lips would follow, I'm not sure why, I just think when you love someone, you want to kiss them everywhere. I enjoy feeling, tasting, becoming one with this woman I loved. The fire would build. We'd be wanting each other pretty bad by now, but somehow I think we'd know that the slower we went, the better," his voice caught, realizing he was making love with his voice now, he heard his throat constrict into a low groan. "By then, her hips would come up and offer themselves to me. Of their own free will. I'd meet her half way. But I still wouldn't rush her. I'd want to be sure she was ready, sure she was as on fire as I was. If she wasn't, I'd kiss her...there, until she was. There's a special part of a woman that a man can set her on fire. Please her no end. And I'd touch her there with my lips, very carefully, softly. Because I've waited a lifetime for her, and I love her so much."

Hannah gasped. It sounded very much as though she were going through some emotions of her own.

"Don't be embarrassed, by my words, Hannah. God put us on earth to make love and be happy. Making love isn't something dirty or ugly like you see on TV. I think it must be the best thing this side of heaven. In my way of thinkin', God took one of Adam's ribs to make Eve because he knew they would be one and the same. They would love each other."

"You make it sound… lovely." She sighed.

He smiled.

"And then..." his voice was ragged, raw, and needy. "We'd come together in an explosion of love making. I wouldn't stop until I had completely satisfied her. And I'd know I had by the sound of her voice, the beat of her heart, the way she strained against me. Even then, our bodies would rock in unison, until we both collapsed. In total pleasure. Until there was no more energy to touch, feel or taste, only then I'd kiss her and tell her how incredible she was. Then...I'd hold her in my arms and never let her go. And later...maybe the next day, I'd tell her."

"Tell her what?" Hannah's voice rose with such anticipation she sounded as though she had been through the experience with Rusty.

"I'd tell her how much I loved her."

There was a long silence, a little heavy breathing, then a sigh. Rusty smiled to himself, he was exhausted, as though he'd been through this with Hannah just now and felt almost as satisfied as he knew he would if he had.

"She'd be a very lucky girl, Rusty." Hannah said breathlessly.

"And he'd be ten feet tall, if she said she loved him back...." Rusty added.

Hannah sat up in the bed, and spoke very softly, she turned her head to look over at him. "Thanks for sharing that with me."

"Do you think I did it right, Hannah?"

"Very right."

"Night Little Darlin'."

"Night..."

# *Chapter Eleven*

The next day was filled with sight-seeing and Hannah was glad she had dressed casually and worn comfortable shoes. They had walked across the Hoover Dam, taken in a show, gone to an art museum, and now, after watching the water show at the Bellagio, were on their way to eat at Osteria del Circo. Rusty claimed this restaurant was the best in Vegas and they had to try it.

But as they were going into the restaurant, a man came up to them and intruded.

"Hannah? Is that you? My God, but you look wonderful. That hot Texas sun has done wonders for you. You look better than ever. What in the world are you doing here though?"

Hannah opened her mouth, but nothing came out. What were the chances in a city this big and busy of running into Vic?

Rusty glanced first at her, then at the man. "Who is this?"

"Vic Trusdale, meet my husband, Rusty Travers." Hannah said finally finding her voice and pleading with Rusty with her eyes to understand.

"Vic..."

"Husband?" Vic repeated.

Rusty eyed the man up and down. He had to give Hannah credit, the man was immaculate, handsome, and filled out his suit to the T. But why was he here, in Vegas?

"We were about to get our table; would you join us?" Rusty put on his manners, unable to assimilate all this news at once.

"Why thank you, yes, it appears I've a lot of catching up to do with Hannah. So how long have you two been...."

"We're on our honeymoon," Rusty jumped to explain. He didn't like the way the man pulled out the chair for Hannah. That was his job. He didn't like that perfect smile he kept flashing either. He felt his hand itch to wipe that smile away.

"Oh," Vic adjusted his tie, and then ran his hand through his short cropped blonde hair. "I'm sorry to intrude. Maybe another time, then."

"Don't be silly," Hannah rushed to say. She had to keep Vic around until she fully explained the situation to Rusty. Alone she might break down and cry or something. She saw the frown on Rusty's face at Vic's every gesture and knew he didn't like this sudden intrusion any more than she did.

"Yes," Rusty glared at her. "Please join us."

"Alright," Vic smiled and ordered a drink for himself when the waiter came.

Although the Italian meal was delicious, Hannah was sure she didn't taste a bite as she slowly began to explain her connection to Vic and Vegas. Rusty's brows went up a time or two and then he was very quiet while Vic tried to persuade Hannah to come back to his show.

"I'm afraid not. I'm married now. I'm a rancher. My dancing days are over."

"What a shame. She was very good you know." Vic offered as he slicked his blond hair back from his face, and Rusty got a whiff of his bold cologne. The man must have bathed in the darn stuff, he thought to himself. And Hannah likes this kind of man? It didn't seem to fit.

"No, I really didn't know." Rusty said blatantly, but Vic didn't seem to catch the sarcasm.

"Only problem with Hannah was the costumes."

"The costumes?" Rusty questioned looking from one to the other.

Hannah colored.

"Yes, she hated the ones that were topless. Refused to wear them. She was such a great dancer, but she wouldn't wear the costumes. So, we had to write in her numbers. Now that she's married, maybe that has changed?" Vic glanced at Hannah provocatively.

Rusty stood up, unable to stomach the man's insinuations any longer. "I'm sorry friend, but my wife and I are on our honeymoon, and we'd like a little privacy, if you don't mind. Do you think we could talk business another time?"

"Of course, I'm sorry. Another time, Hannah." Vic winked and got up from the table.

"That was rude.... don't you think?" Hannah insisted, sipping her wine a little too quickly.

"Maybe, but he didn't seem to get the hint. Now, suppose you tell me why you neglected to tell me about working here in Vegas. It seems I've been making a fool out of myself showing you around a town you know more about than I do." Rusty demanded biting into his garlic bread with relish.

Hannah chuckled, and then broke out in a laugh. The wine was getting to her. It felt so warm, so cozy.

"I've been terrified ever since I found out we were coming here." She laughed.

"And that's funny?"

"No, but it's silly. I mean, what were the chances of bumping into Vic? And then we did. I'm sorry..." she gazed into Rusty's eyes and her expression softened. "I should have told you. I just didn't know how."

"You sure didn't mind letting me make a fool of myself." He berated, some of his anger dissipated.

She placed her hand over his...."You didn't make a fool of yourself. I've enjoyed every single moment of it. I want you to understand something." She looked into his eyes now, unable to look away. "I worked here, Rusty. I never had time to enjoy it. I busted my butt trying to get my brother through school and send Dad some money too. This wasn't some luxurious vacation for me. I came here with the intention of working. I got lucky and got a job almost immediately. I didn't have professional training of any sort. Vic said I was a natural, but it didn't come that easy. I worked, 10 to twelve hours a day, on my feet. And then I had to wear these skimpy little outfits that barely covered me. But that wasn't the worst." She stopped, hiccupped and pleaded with him with her eyes. "No, the worst was the way the men would stare, and gawk at me. And think so little of me. I hated it. I'd never want to go back to doing this kind of work again."

She hiccupped again. He blinked.

She was inebriated. He suddenly realized he needed to get her home in bed. He paid their tab, and took her elbow, gently guiding her out of the restaurant. She could barely walk straight.

When they finally arrived at the hotel, she staggered at the elevator, he picked her up in his arms and carried her to the room. He took her to the bed, laid her down, and took off her shoes. Then pulled the sheet up over her.

She gazed up at him with a sleepy expression. "You're wonderful.... you know."

He nodded and smiled. "Yeah, sure...a real gentleman."

"Hmm..." she said and rolled over and went to sleep.

He sat down on the bed opposite her and stared at her long and hard, at her small little frame in that big bed, alone.

She had been a dancer! And now he knew her secrets and he'd never mention them again, and she'd never dance again, except in his arms, he decided.

He heard her snore and smiled. "Sleep Little Darlin'."

*****

The next morning, she wasn't feeling too well, and Rusty had a Bloody Mary, and a wash cloth ready for her. After pampering her for a while, he ordered their breakfast and took a quick shower while she tried to snap out of it. But Hannah had never had a hang-over before and she didn't realize that loud noises like running water, knocks at the door, and sunlight would nearly kill her.

Throwing a robe on when the waiter arrived with room service, she readied Rusty's chair around the small table by the patio door. She glanced out, but the sun seemed so bright and hurt her eyes. She pulled the curtain. It made the room dark again. She sighed. The water turned off, she sighed again. The waiter went away and didn't slam the door this time. Thank God for little miracles.

Rusty was fully dressed when he came in the room and noted the darkness.

"Looks good," he quipped, his eyes going over first her, then the food. If he was thinking she was pitiful he didn't say, and she was grateful.

Hannah wore a pair of jeans that actually fit that she had bought in Vegas, and a shirt that Rusty had picked out for her and flattered her figure. Rusty seemed appreciative, although with a scowl on his face it was hard to tell.

"Hungry?" She asked trying to break the sudden ice in the room.

"Sure," he cut into his French toast. "Did you sleep well?"

Hannah sighed, and turned away so he couldn't see her expression. "It was a comfortable bed. Did you?"

"Like a baby," he growled.

"I'm glad you were comfortable," she smiled brightly irritated that he had gotten a good night sleep, when she couldn't remember a thing.

"Comfortable, yes..." He began but didn't finish.

"I see you like French toast," she giggled as he grabbed a couple more pieces and put them on his plate.

Then she grabbed her head and hung on for dear life as the sound of her own laughter hurt so badly.

"So... what are we going to do today?"

He opened his mouth to reply but her cell phone rang. They both glared at the intrusion.

She grabbed it off the kitchen counter and answered it with a puzzled expression on her face.

"Yes, he's here, just a minute...." Hannah handed the phone to Rusty. "I think it's Deke."

"Better get your butt back here, bro." Deke's voice sounded agitated.

"What? Do you realize I'm on a honeymoon? What's wrong now?" Rusty countered just as unpleasantly.

"Jennifer's here. She says she's pregnant!" Deke declared.

Rusty's face contorted, then with a heavy sigh he added, "So....?"

"She says it's yours!"

Rusty nearly dropped the phone. He stared at it for a long moment. He glanced at Hannah who was staring at him with questions in her eyes. "I'll have to check the weather forecast. We'll be there as soon as we can."

"Good. The sooner you straighten this out, the better." Deke declared in an angry tone.

It was obvious his brother thought it was true. And if Deke thought that, so would Hannah.

"Something wrong?" Hannah asked innocently.
"We've got to get back. Something has come up."

Rusty said, not wanting to go into detail until he had time to think. What was Jennifer up to? With worry dogging him, he glanced at Hannah's face, and saw the disappointment. He felt it too. He knew he had gotten to her the night before. Not only that, but knowing now what her big secret was, he felt he could finally at last trust her with anything. Anything that is...but this.

He knew after his confession that they had a chance at making this a real marriage, given the proper time. But how was he gonna make it work with Jennifer pulling stunts like this. He had to straighten her out and fast. Before he lost the one thing, he didn't want to lose.... Hannah!

After calling the weather station, and the airport, he packed their things and they headed out. The trip home was almost in silence and Hannah seemed puzzled.

"Is everything okay at the ranch?" Hannah asked when he didn't furnish her any information.

"Yeah, the ranch is fine. It's something I have to take care of." Rusty explained.

"Alright," Hannah nodded and didn't ask any more questions. Still the tension rose between them with every mile closer to home. Whatever he had accomplished with Hannah in Vegas was quickly being destroyed by the problem at hand. He wanted to tell her, but he wasn't that sure of how she'd react. And he wouldn't blame her.

Rusty tried to be considerate, tried to pay attention to Hannah, but his mind was full of problems. Why had Jennifer named him the father? Who was the father? And why now of all times?

It was a couple of hours later before they landed safely on a private airstrip and was greeted by Deke and Emma. Emma looked worried, Deke looked mad, and Rusty's nerves were stretched as far as a man could stretch them.

Deke had brought Rusty's truck and Emma had driven their truck. Emma directed Hannah to the other truck and Hannah looked perplexed by the sudden separation. She glanced at Rusty, but he nodded.

"Go with Emma, honey. I've got some business to attend to. I'll be home soon." He promised.

Hannah nodded and sat woodenly on the passenger side, watching Rusty and Deke drive off in a hurry. That's when she got a gut full of fears that something was drastically wrong.

"Do you know what's going on, Emma?" Hannah asked innocently.

Emma started the truck and nodded. "I know a little. But I think this is one Rusty is going to have to explain to you himself."

"Can't you at least give me some hint as to what's going on?" Hannah begged, feeling an uneasiness creeping over her. She hadn't felt this way since...Jennifer!

Oh no, it was Jennifer. She just knew it was. But what was wrong now?

"It's Jennifer, isn't it?" Hannah tried to sound calm.

Emma glanced at her warily. "Yes, it's Jennifer."

Hannah dreaded hearing this acknowledgement.

Just knowing that Jennifer was still important enough to Rusty to intrude on their honeymoon made it ultra-clear to Hannah that Jennifer was still a very big part of Rusty's life. Whether he admitted it to himself or not.

She'd been so convinced that he was over her. Now this....

Somehow, she had to be levelheaded about it all. But how? Her husband was going to meet with another woman, at this very minute and there was nothing she could do to stop it.

It seemed so out of place to want to stop him, but she did. She loved him, and she really wanted to stop him from going to Jennifer.

"I'm sure it's all just a big mistake." Emma said meekly. Obviously, Emma was uncomfortable in this situation.

Hannah nodded. She refused to think about this. She had no idea what Jennifer was up to except trying to keep Rusty for herself. Maybe Rusty wanted to be fought over. Maybe he enjoyed this kind of thing. Maybe this was all to make Jennifer jealous. She could maybe it all to death. She wanted answers and Emma wasn't the one to give them to her.

*****

"Why the hell didn't you tell me about you and Jennifer?" Deke demanded as they spun off the airstrip and onto the highway. Deke's hands gripped the steering wheel so tight, Rusty knew it was his neck he was wringing.

"What's to tell?" Rusty asked angered that his brother had assumed the worst in him.

"For God's sake, getting her pregnant, and then marrying Hannah. Have you lost your mind? Why didn't you just face up to your responsibilities and marry Jennifer?" Deke asked his foot accelerating.

Rusty firmed his lips and held back his anger. This wasn't Deke's fault. "Did it ever occur to you or anyone else for that matter, that the baby isn't mine?"

Deke's glance whipped about to stare into his brother's eyes. "Are you telling me, it isn't yours?"

"You're damn right I am..." Rusty's spat out. "I told you a long time ago that Jennifer and I hadn't been doing anything. I meant it."

Deke braked the truck, nearly causing Rusty to hit the dash. He grabbed for him and shook himself. "Dammit bro, I'm sorry. I jumped to the wrong conclusion. I didn't want to believe it, but you guys went together so long, and it seemed as though you were marrying Hannah to make Jennifer jealous. Obviously, I've got it all wrong. So, level, what is going on here?"

Rusty's anger seemed to spin in every direction, except at Deke. He didn't blame his brother, he knew how persuasive Jennifer could be. But he wanted the same answers Deke did. And he wanted to get back to Hannah before someone told her.

"What's happening is...I've fallen in love with Hannah, and Jennifer is throwing kinks in every move I make." Then taking a breath he asked. "So, where's Jennifer now?"

"She's home, at her folk's house. I told her I'd bring you there, as soon as I could. Sounds like someone's got a lot of explaining to do."

When Deke drove into Jennifer's folk's yard, Rusty opened his door to get out.

"Looks like everyone's gone to bed." Deke nodded toward the house.

"Then we'll just have to wake them up, won't we?" Rusty said, his voice sneering at the darkness.

The sound of heavy boots crunching on the porch woke someone and a light came on. Jennifer stood in the doorway. Even with disheveled hair, no make-up and an old robe on Jennifer looked like a model. She also looked worried. She glanced almost guiltily at Rusty, then Deke.

"Thanks Deke," Jennifer said as though she'd been waiting all day for Rusty to come, and she was dismissing Deke altogether.

Deke started to walk off, but Rusty pulled at his jacket sleeve.

"No, I want you to hear this. I want you to witness it." Rusty said and walked into the house as though he'd been invited in.

Deke hesitated then followed.

Jennifer seemed upset that Deke was staying, but she said nothing and followed them inside.

The house was a comfortable old two-story farm house that her grandfather had built several decades before. It was modest, but clean, Rusty mused as he turned all his attention on Jennifer.

"Would you like some coffee?" She asked Rusty then Deke. Both men shook their heads.

"No, we'd like the truth. We both know I'm not the father." Rusty raised his voice just a tad.

"I know this was kind of a dirty trick, getting you back from your honeymoon so soon, but I have no one to turn to, but you, Rusty...!" Jennifer cried, real tears rolling down her cheek.

Rusty hated when women cried. It made him feel responsible.

"If you want my help you better tell my brother I'm not the father, and now!" Rusty exploded.

Jennifer saw the anger in his eyes and nodded, the tears didn't go away. Instead she broke down and wept on Rusty's shoulder.

"I went to work in Dallas. It seemed like a nice company. Only...some of the girls—well they were going to weekend parties with some of the male employees. That didn't seem so bad, so I went along. Swimming, dancing, lots of fun. Brad was so nice to me, at first. He would send me gifts, take me to exotic places. Then I found out he was still married and that his wife was pregnant. I was jealous. I loved him by then. She wouldn't give him a divorce, so he said. So..." she glanced at Rusty with pleading eyes. "I decided if I got pregnant, he'd leave her and come to me. He wanted more children. It didn't work out that way. He said he loved his wife, and thought I understood it. He won't divorce her. I left, came home. It seemed to me as though Deke was forcing you to marry this Hannah, so I decided to name you as the father. I thought it would be a good out, if you wanted out of the marriage Rusty. My family is in shock. I don't have any idea how to tell them the truth. They assumed you were the father, and I'm afraid I let them."

"And did you tell them I was the father?" Rusty bit his lip to keep from reacting.

"Yes...I'm afraid I did. I had too," she pleaded seeing the anger building in Rusty.

"Why?" Rusty shouted.

"I couldn't tell them the truth. It would kill them, Rusty. They could accept you getting me pregnant after all, we'd been together so long. But a stranger...they'd die of embarrassment." Jennifer pleaded.

Rusty started for the door, "Then I suggest you tell them the truth, now."

"I can't...." Jennifer shook her head, her make-up running down her cheek convinced Rusty the tears were real, but he refused to bail Jennifer out of this one. "Please don't ask it of me, not yet..."

"You'd better and you'd better do it fast." Rusty shouted.

Deke moved between them. "Jennifer, maybe I could tell them."

"Oh no... you can't. I can't do that to them...." she begged and pleaded with her eyes going to Rusty.

"Maybe you should have thought of that sooner, Jennifer." Rusty said, disgusted with her pleads.

"You don't love Hannah, do you?" Jennifer cried as though it might be her last straw.

There was a prolonged silence, and then Rusty looked Deke in the eye, "More every day I'm with her."

Jennifer hung her head. Then glancing at Deke, she added, "But I thought this was all just a marriage of convenience."

"It started out that way, but not any longer." Rusty affirmed. "I'm sorry for you Jennifer but the sooner you straighten this out, the better."

"I can't. I won't!" Jennifer cried.

"Then I will!" Rusty vowed. "In fact, maybe tonight wouldn't be too soon."

"Oh please, don't. Don't do this, Rusty."

Deke grabbed Rusty's arm, "It'll keep another day." Rusty stared at Jennifer. "You tell them tomorrow, or I will."

Then Rusty and Deke left, spinning out of the yard and sending the dirt flying.

"Do you think she'll tell them?" Deke asked as they drove toward the ranch.

"I don't know. But she better. God, I can't believe she was so stupid." Rusty shook his head and banged his fist against the dash. "Dammit Deke, I never touched her, ever! All that preaching you did, sunk in. I decided I'd be one Travers that didn't jump the gun. I even thought of myself as a little noble. Of course, I knew I'd be ribbed if I confessed, but this would make any man confess his sins."

"I'm damn glad you listened, bro. But now you better calm down before we get home. I'm sure Hannah still has no idea what is wrong." Deke reminded him.

Rusty quieted.

That night Rusty held Hannah close, kissed her goodnight and watched Emma follow her to a bedroom. He'd be sleeping on the couch. Not exactly what he'd planned, but this wasn't the time to make love to his wife. Not until he had this mess straightened out.

He just wished he could be sure Jennifer would tell her folks!

*****

Emma took Hannah into town the next day, while Rusty helped Deke mend a couple of fences. Deke called it therapy, Rusty called it avoiding the inevitable.

Emma had to pick up some supplies and Hannah seemed happy to get away from the tension building at the ranch.

There hadn't been any private time with Rusty, so she didn't know any more about the problem than she had the night before. No one was talking. And something within her was kind of glad they weren't. She had a strange feeling she wouldn't like what they might tell her.

Concentrating on Emma's grocery list, she couldn't help but overhear a nearby conversation.

"Emma, I guess you've heard." A strange voice in the next aisle exclaimed.

"Heard what?" Emma asked innocently.

"Jennifer's gonna have Rusty's baby, of course. Don't tell me you didn't know. Oh, we know about that gal he married over by Pecos, but Jennifer said that was just a ruse. Said her and Rusty never stopped lovin' each other. 'Course we all knew they hadn't. Rusty has always been crazy about our Jenny. Guess it was a might hard on the gal though. How'd she take it?"

Hannah didn't realize her eyes were full of unshed tears as she listened. Her sudden gasp and hiccup brought Emma around the aisle and to her side.

"Don't listen to them, Hannah." Emma encouraged.

"Why didn't he tell me?" Hannah asked, not really seeing Emma at all.

"He hasn't had much of a chance...." Emma tried to take up for Rusty the only way she knew how.

"He's had the time. He could have told me in the plane coming home. He's lied to me. Oh Emma, I'm such a fool."

"No, you aren't." Emma grabbed her and hugged her to her. "I'm sure Rusty can straighten this all out, just give him a chance."

"I should have known." Hannah cried out.

"Give him a chance to explain, honey." Emma encouraged. "It's probably just a big misunderstanding."

Hannah pulled away. She stared into Emma's face and shook her head. "I need to go home. Can you help me get out of here...today!"

"Hannah, you've got to give Rusty a chance to explain this. It's not fair..."

"I can't...you don't understand...he lied to me...he told me..." she stopped and shook her head again, this time letting the tears fall. "I've got to get out of here."

Emma nodded, paid for her groceries and drove Hannah away from the grocery store.

"Emma can you drive me home?"

"Well I..." she glanced at the distraught figure beside her and nodded. "Yes, of course I can. I'll have to make a few phone calls, make sure someone picks Sammie Jo up from school. I'm sure Cal will watch the baby. Okay, relax, I'll drive you home. It's the least I can do. But are you sure you don't want to sit down with Rusty and talk this out, first?"

"I can't. Please understand."

"I do, Hannah, I do." Emma nodded, but the worried look didn't leave her face.

"Have you considered it might be Jennifer lying?"

"Why would she lie about something like that?"

"I don't know. I was asleep when Deke and Rusty came in last night, and I didn't talk to either of them this morning before they left, so I don't know. But I do know them both, very well, and I know Rusty isn't a liar."

Hannah folded and refolded a Kleenex that Emma handed her, wanting to believe Emma, but knowing it would be futile. Rusty had told her only a few nights ago that he was a virgin, and now this.

To lie like that...just to get her in his bed...or his heart, or both!

She couldn't forgive that!

It was a long drive and both women were exhausted by the time they reached Hannah's house. Hannah insisted Emma stay the night and leave the next day. Emma had called Deke and told him not to mention where they were to Rusty at Hannah's request.

"What are you going to do Hannah?" Emma asked the next morning before leaving her.

"I'm going to go back to work and pay for this ranch, the way I should have all along. I owe Rusty and I aim to pay him back."

"But the deadline is this week, what will you do?" "I don't know. Maybe I'll lose this place. Maybe it's a lost cause."

"Hannah don't talk like that."

"Please," Hannah touched Emma's arm as she was about to drive away, "Don't tell Rusty what I'm going to do. I don't want him feeling guilty about it. It's not his fault. This ranch is my problem."

Emma grimaced, "And Rusty?"

"Rusty will be just fine. He can have our marriage annulled I'll sign the papers, and then he can marry Jennifer and make things right." Hannah smiled sadly. "The way they should have been all along."

"You mean...you didn't." Emma intimated what she was talking about.

"No... we didn't."

"Maybe you should have." Emma said quite frankly.

"Emma!"

"Might have solved a lot of trouble." Emma nodded with a faint smile to her lips.

"I made a mistake, Emma. I fell in love with him." Hannah admitted. "But...please don't tell him."

"But...Hannah," Emma fretted.

"Please."

"Alright, Hannah, if that's what you want. I really liked having a ranch savvy sister-in-law. I'll miss you Hannah." Emma choked.

"Ditto," cried Hannah and waved her goodbye. She remembered the line from the movie.

*****

"What do you mean she's gone. Where did she go?"

Rusty demanded as Deke tried to calm his brother down as Deke hung up the phone. "Emma took her home."

Deke explained, pouring a large glass of milk for his brother.

"Home! Why?" Rusty demanded standing up and facing his brother.

"She knows...." that was all Deke said.

"Knows! Who the hell told her?" Rusty shouted, grabbing his head as though it were about to come off his shoulders and he had to hold it on.

"Jennifer's folks."

"When did she run into them?" Rusty demanded.

"When Emma took her to town this morning. Look, I'm no happier about this than you, but face it brother. This is a lot for any woman to take. Leave her be. Let her think this out, she can hear you out later. First you have to get over there and tell Jennifer's parents the truth before they spread this all over the place."

"I have to! That's not my job."

"Unless you want them telling the whole community that you and Jennifer are having a child together, you better set them straight. It sure doesn't look as though she plans on doing it any time soon." Deke declared, glaring at his brother.

Rusty flopped into the chair and gulped the milk down. "Hell's bells, how could anything get so screwed up?"

"I don't know...I just don't know."

"I need to talk to Hannah..."

"Agreed, but not tonight. Tonight, you need to talk to Jennifer and her folks. Get this thing taken care of before it blows wide open. Then you can talk to Hannah." Deke advised.

Rusty agreed but decided to have one more glass of milk before taking care of it.

*****

It hadn't been easy. Jennifer stalled him as long as possible before Rusty finally approached the subject. At first Jennifer's father was adamant that Rusty was lying. Jennifer finally admitted the truth and it took hours to calm them down. Her mother cried for what seemed like hours to Rusty.

"Why didn't you tell us?" her father asked, shaking his head with tears in his eyes.

"I couldn't hurt you. You had so much faith in me. I couldn't destroy that. But on the other hand, I couldn't continue to let you think Rusty was the father either. It seems, Rusty is in love with his wife." Jennifer announced stonily.

"Does she know?" Jennifer's mother asked innocently and Rusty realized quickly where Jennifer got that trait.

"She overheard you talking to Emma," Rusty informed her not too sweetly.

"Oh, dear God, I'm sorry for that."

"Me too," Rusty reflected. Conjuring Hannah in his mind he could see her tears, her hurt. He needed to be with her...not Jennifer!

"A man should be responsible for bringing a child into the world. He should have known better." Jennifer's father shook his head again, his sorrow multiplied with anger.

"I should have too, Dad." Jennifer said, drying her tears and glancing at Rusty. "I'm sorry Rusty. I'm sorry I involved you. I just thought.... maybe...."

Rusty knew what she thought. If it hadn't been for Hannah, he might have rushed to save Jennifer, but he loved Hannah. And that's where his loyalties lay.

"I'd better go," Rusty finally said, satisfied that everyone knew and understood now.

Jennifer rose from the couch. "I'll walk you out." It was a quiet night; a hint of spring was in the air.

Bluebonnets would line the hills before long. The long cold winter was almost over.

"I really didn't know...." Jennifer began in a low throaty voice.

"Know what?" Rusty asked distracted.

"That you loved her." Jennifer said almost painfully.

"Yeah, I do."

"Will she understand?" Jennifer asked hopefully.

Rusty glanced at her and smiled sadly, "I don't know. Would you?"

"That's a good question." Jennifer nodded.

Then as Rusty climbed into his pickup, Jennifer threw her arms around his neck and pulled him through the open windshield. "Good luck."

"Thanks," Rusty nodded, and sped out of the yard as quickly as possible.

It was late, he was tired, and yet he knew he should go after Hannah. Still a good night's sleep would allow him a clearer head and less chance of an accident. So, he headed back to the 4 Bar None.

There was a light on and as he opened the back-kitchen door, he saw his father sitting at the kitchen table. It was like Cal Travers to wait up for his sons, when they were in trouble. He was like a rock, always there for them.

"Get things straightened out?" Cal asked nonchalantly as though he weren't concerned, and yet he was.

Rusty wanted to laugh. His father was worried. Worried just like he had a million times when his kids had come home with a weighty problem on their shoulders. Cal was there for them, all of them. And he was always on their side.

"With Jennifer and her folks. Yeah." Rusty said quietly.

"Good. What about Hannah?"

Rusty sat down at the table, ran his finger over the top of the sugar bowl and glanced at his dad with worried eyes.

"I don't know, dad. I've got to go talk to her. But I decided to wait until morning. I'm pretty beat, and I need a clear head when I try to explain all this to her."

Cal nodded, "Now that's good thinking, son. I was a little worried you'd go after her tonight. That's not wise."

Rusty smiled. "Do you think she'll understand?"

"I don't know son. If she really loves you, then yes, I do."

"And if she doesn't?"

"You know the answer to that."

"If only I'd told her about it on the way home. We could have talked it out, and there wouldn't have been a problem." Rusty acknowledged.

"Maybe, but I'm sure you were still in a state of shock when you flew home. Deke has a way of springing things that is to be desired. Still, he means well."

"I know." Rusty rubbed the stubble on his chin. He took his hat off, ran his fingers over his face and looked up at his dad.

"You really love her, don't you?" Cal's eyes sparkled into his son's.

"Yes, I do." Rusty declared. "And dad, just so you know, it's kind of like the love you had for mother. Before I knew she was beautiful I loved her, after, I loved her in spite of the fact that she was. It's real dad, and I can't lose her."

"Then you go after her, tell her the truth and make her listen." Cal said getting up from the table.

"There's apple pie in the fridge if you want some. Emma made it tonight." Cal said walking away.

Rusty didn't hear him, he had fallen asleep at the table.

*****

But the next morning things didn't get any better. Deke had been trying to bust a bronc in the corral and got thrown against the barn. His leg was broken, and he'd be laid up for a while. Rusty knew there was no one to help but himself. His dad couldn't carry on at the ranch alone. Clint had new responsibilities and Jake was in Peaceful. It was up to him.

"Don't worry, Deke. I'll stay until you mend." Rusty declared that morning after bringing Deke home from the emergency room in Sweetwater.

"I'd appreciate it, might give Hannah some thinking time too. Have you called her?"

"I tried, a dozen times. She's not answering." Rusty looked away, his exasperation getting the better of him.

"Keep trying," Emma urged.

"I will. Well, better get out to the north pasture, make sure the water holes aren't frozen. You gonna be alright?" Rusty asked as his brother winced from moving his leg just a tad to the footstool.

"I'll be fine. Sorry about all this bro..."

"It'll keep," he mumbled and went out the door. But would it? Would Hannah listen to him when he finally could get to her?

*****

"What do you mean, Josey, she's gone?" Rusty demanded as he spoke through the screen door of the bunkhouse.

"I mean she packed up and left last week." Josey said as her sister came to stand beside her.

Rusty looked at the other woman, and not recognizing her twisted his head as if to ask.

"Oh, this is my sister, Katie." Josey explained. "She's staying with me until I get word from Hannah on what to do with things here. We'll be out of here by next week. They foreclosed.... you know."

Rusty nodded. "I saw it boarded up. When will she be back?" Rusty asked.

"Don't know. Said when they delivered the papers to get an apartment in town and write her." Josey said.

"Write her where?" Rusty demanded.

"I don't know.... I mean.... well, I guess she's gone back to Vegas." Josey said throwing her hands in the air in exasperation. "Said something about paying you back."

"Vegas!" Rusty boomed.

Josey eyed him closely. "Said she was gonna earn the money to pay for this place or lose it, but she wouldn't be beholdin' to any man."

"Beholdin'?"

"That was her words alright." Josey nodded.

Rusty backed away from the screen, ran a hand through his hair and put his hat back on his head. "I've got to find her Josey. I've got to."

"Yes sir, I can see that." Josey nodded, a slow smile curling her lips.

"Thanks...." Rusty said, starting to walk off.

"Where you goin'?" Josey asked.

"To see Mr. Simmons and straighten out all the paper work, then to bring her home."

Josey laughed out loud, "Yes siree, that's good. It sure is!"

Rusty headed for Pecos.

Katie turned to Josey, "Now who on earth was that man?"

Josey laughed, threw her arm around her little sister and replied, "Why honey, that was Hannah's Man!"

# *Chapter Twelve*

"Mr. Simmons?" Rusty approached the banker with all the confidence in the world.

"Aw...Mr. Travers. How nice to see you? What can I do for you? I got the paperwork drawn up just as you requested. All I need is your signature." the banker said as though they were old friends.

Remembering the last time, he was in the bank, Rusty almost shook his head, but knew that business was business.

"I'll take care of that formality right now. And you did as I requested and put it in both our names, right?" Rusty said pointing to the office they had used the last time.

"Mr. Rusty Travers and Mrs. Hannah Travers, as you requested." Mr. Simmons motioned.

"I suppose this is sorta like a wedding present then for her...?"

"Absolutely." Rusty explained. "We'll need her signature too."

"You'll have it in a few days, I promise." Rusty nodded and signed the document.

"Well, it's a pleasure doing business with you Mr. Travers. I hope our association will be long and fruitful?" Mr. Simmons asked.

Rusty shook his hand and walked out into the sunlight.

At least he had stood firm and convinced Simmons of his intentions. Now to convince Hannah!

*****

Hannah adjusted her headset again for the fourth time. She hadn't remembered just how heavy they sometimes were. Following directions, she had only messed up twice, but according to Vic, that was two too many times. He expected her to be in the line-up tonight, and she was not prepared to go back on so soon. Every part of her body screamed that she wasn't ready for a performance yet.

"That was pretty good, but you've got to do better." Vic said coming up to her and handing her a towel.

"I'm trying. It's been a while." She reasoned mopping her forehead with the towel and rubbing her legs against the cramps that threatened each time she practiced.

Vic pulled her off the stage, took her in his arms and kissed her. She didn't respond. She felt like a piece of wood, unmoved by any emotion except pure exhaustion. He looked into her eyes and frowned.

"Did you go and fall for that cowboy?" Vic asked backing away from her, so he could look at her.

Hannah hung her head. She didn't want to think about Rusty. It was still much too painful. All she wanted was to dance, make money, and somehow, get her ranch back, if that were possible.

Exhaustion made her moody and she answered angrily. "I came back to dance Vic. That's all. But don't butt into my private life."

"Okay, fine, so dance. Quit falling on your face out there and dance. Show me what you've got. Only if you can't cut it, just say the word. Get out now. I'm not babysitting a love-sick cowgirl. Make up your mind what you want, Hannah."

"I told you what I want. I want to work." She protested as her leg nearly folded under her.

"Alright. Then practice until you're good again." He instructed and walked away.

Until she was good again? Did that mean she was bad? Oh, she knew she was out of shape, but was she really that bad? She couldn't be. She had to push herself to make it. She had to work until she couldn't stand, let alone dance.

With that firmly planted in her mind, she began to rehearse again. Still, she faltered on some steps. She silently scolded herself, wondering why she had suddenly become almost clumsy.

Out of shape, her mind reeled. She had to get 'into shape'.

One, two, three, four, pivot, turn, walk, then glide like an angel. Oh, she could do this. Couldn't she?

The lights bore down on her and she felt the sweat peppering her forehead and upper lip. She felt like a pig. Thinking of that made her homesick. She couldn't concentrate on the ranch right now. Right now, she had to concentrate on the dance.

The other girls watched on the sidelines as she practiced and wondered why she worked so hard. Before it had come natural to her, now she had to work at it.

"You'll never have to work there again," rang Rusty's words in her head.

She had to forget Rusty. He had been wrong. He had lied to her, and she had to forget him.

As she moved and glided across the floor her mind drifted off and suddenly the choreographer was standing before her.

"What are you doing?"

"W-what?" she asked coming out of her reverie.

"That wasn't the move you were supposed to make. What are you thinking?"

"I'm sorry!" She shouted. "I'm tired. I need to rest."

"You go on tonight. You can't rest." he insisted.

Can't rest, can't rest! Her mind was screaming at her to run away from here, but she knew she had to stay. She had to see this through.

"Now...again!" came the call from the distance.

This time she did better. But her legs were cramping, and she would have to rest soon, or she would never go on.

The costume director came on stage and handed her the costume for tonight's number.

She shrieked. "No... I can't wear this! It must be a mistake."

From out of nowhere Vic appeared. "Oh yes you will. You wanted a job, you got one. But you will work for it, and you will wear this costume."

"I-I can't, Vic. You know I can't."

"What? It's against your religion?" he asked sarcastically.

"Maybe it is...." she said dejectedly.

He shook his head. "You wear this costume, or you don't go on...ever!"

"Then she won't go on...ever!" came a voice from the darkness of the theater.

Everyone turned around trying to find the voice. "Who's out there?" Vic called, shading his eyes from the stage lights to see.

Hannah didn't have to, she recognized that voice. Her head flew up, and tears welled in her eyes. It was Rusty. He was here!

"Rusty Travers, Hannah's husband, if you recall!"

Hannah came forward just a little.

"And I say if she dances, she'll wear this costume, and be glad of it. Now what do you say Hannah?"

Hannah saw Rusty approach the bottom of the stage stairs. She felt her heartbeat quicken. Her palms sweat, her mind went into overdrive. How could she answer? How could she take her eyes from the one man who meant so much to her?

"I-I"

"She won't be dancing for you anymore..." Rusty said calmly. "She's coming home, with me."

Hannah stared at Rusty as though he weren't real. There he stood in all his splendor, the cowboy. He wore fitted jeans, a chambray shirt with a brown corduroy jacket and that ever famous brown felt hat. He looked good enough to eat. Every fiber of her being strained to go to him, but she fought it.

Then sanity prevailed, and she found her voice again. "Rusty, I've got to do this. Please, don't interfere. Just go home."

Rusty bowed his head a moment, then raised his chin defiantly, "And exactly where is my home, now Hannah?"

Hannah stared into his beautiful blue eyes one last time, before bowing her head, "The 4 Bar None."

"Is that the way you really want it?" Rusty asked.

Hannah hesitated, wishing she could run to him, and beg him to stay with her. But she nodded.

"We've got things to talk about Hannah. And I'm not leaving until we've talked them out." Rusty persisted.

Hannah walked slowly up to him, so close she could smell the faint odor of his woodsy cologne, feel the warmth of his breath against her cheek as he spoke, so close she could almost feel the smooth of his cheek. "I'm sorry, but I think you better leave."

Rusty stared long and hard at her, and then walked slowly back the way he had come. Hannah stared after him, unaware that tears were falling down her cheek.

Some of the other dancers came up to her and tried to comfort her, but she insisted she was okay and that she had to get back to work.

Hannah ignored the fact that she wouldn't wear the costume. Ignored the fact that her heart was breaking and kept on practicing. As though the act of practicing would make the ache inside her go away.

But later that night, she was standing alone in her dressing room and trying to figure out how she would go on stage in that ridiculous costume when Rusty came into the room. He locked the door with a key and turned to face her.

"W-what are you doing here?" she gasped, already drinking in his handsome face. She had long ago memorized that face. Those dark blue eyes that danced when he was teasing, the furrow in his brow when he was worried, the stubborn jut of his chin when he was determined. "How did you get the key?"

"Looks like this is the only way we are gonna talk this out."

"There's nothing to talk about Rusty." Hannah swept past him and tried to unlock the door, but he had taken the key and put it in his pocket.

"Looking for this?" he dangled the key in front of her then put it back in his coat pocket.

"Why did you come here?" she asked.

"To get my wife back." he said simply.

"I can't go back with you Rusty." She waited for that to sink in before she continued. "We were silly to think we could make this work. Jennifer is too much a part of your life. You can't just wipe her out, even if you wanted to. Please...don't make this any harder than it is. Just go home."

"You actually believe I fathered her baby...after what I told you, in Vegas?" He rasped.

Hannah shook her head and turned away, pretending to check the costume. The cold costume glittered, but it held no interest for her.

"It doesn't matter what I believe." she mumbled.

"The hell it doesn't," he rasped, pulling her back around to meet his somber gaze. His fingers burned where he touched her on the arms.

"I wasn't lying to you. I've never touched Jennifer or any woman, Hannah. Not that I don't want to right this minute, but we've got to straighten this out, and now. I didn't mean for it to happen."

Hannah felt hot tears sting her eyes, "Why are you telling me all this? Why do you care what I think?"

A smoldering look crossed his face as he held her at arm's length. Then shook her gently. "Because I love you Hannah O'Leary Travers. Because I didn't lie to you, wouldn't lie to you. And can't live without you."

"B-but...the baby?" Hannah gasped, trying to take in his words and afraid to believe in them.

"Isn't mine. I've never touched Jennifer. She met a man, thought she was in love and got pregnant. Then found out he was married and had no intention of marrying her. The usual story, I guess. It's not mine, Hannah. I never touched her. Won't you believe me?"

"But her parents...."

"Didn't know the truth either. They do now." Rusty's glance went over her thoroughly.

Hannah stood there staring into his eyes, watching the display of lights, and darks in his eyes. And then she knew. He wasn't lying.

A slow burning smile lit her lips, "You love me?"

"With all my heart, Little Darlin'. I want a chance to make this a real marriage Hannah. We've got something very good here. Let's don't lose it." He suggested and pulled her into his waiting arms.

Hannah felt the heat of the moment as her body glided into his arms.

Then suddenly his lips touched hers and she lost all resistance. She loved this man truly and nothing could prevent her from showing him just how much.

"Oh, Rusty....I've missed you so much. I wanted to call...to hear your voice. But I was afraid I'd hear rejection and I couldn't face that. I felt I had no right to come between you and Jennifer."

"I'd never reject you Darlin'. Never." He said in a rough rasp. He held her closely then set her away and stared into her eyes.

Slowly he reached up to stroke her cheek and smile into her tear stained eyes. "Don't cry, Little Darlin'."

"I can't help it. I'm so happy..." she cried

"Me too....me too!" As his lips found hers, she knew instantly that she'd found her man. She knew they would make it together, because they both felt the same about so many things that were important in life.

"But…" she pulled back just a little, "What about Jennifer?"

"What about her?" He asked, intent on destroying all her defenses at once as he kissed her eyes, her nose, her cheek, and then her lips. His tongue sought the sweetness of her own and he groaned as he pulled away just in time.

He had come after her, and now she would go home...with him. But where was home?

"Oh Rusty," she cried pulling out of his arms and pacing. "The ranch...it's gone!"

"Does it matter...I mean, can't we make a home anywhere as long as we're together."

The smile in his eyes promised her heaven, and she nodded without another word and flew into his arms.

"Of course, I'm sorry." she said kissing his neck. His cologne tickled her nose, as she melted in his arms. It was so right, her mind cried.

He kissed her solidly on the lips, then whispered, "Good, now let's get out of here and go home."

She glanced at the sequined dress, "Oh yes, let's."

*****

The Lear jet was nearing the runway in Midland. Hannah was puzzled; she thought they'd be flying to the 4 Bar None.

"Rusty, where are we going?"

"I thought you might want to see the place one last time," he remarked, not looking directly at her.

"Oh, yes, do you think they'd mind?" she asked wistfully.

"They? They who?"

"The ones that bought it?" she quipped.

Rusty glanced at her and quickly glanced away, as though hiding some unknown emotion. "No, I don't think they would."

Rusty rented a car in Midland and they drove out to the old ranch place.

There was no for sale sign up. The boarded-up ranch house was now painted and looking like new. The barn had been repaired too.

Hannah felt the hot tears welling, but she was determined not to let them fall. Instead she made her way toward the small cemetery that her father had created.

She saw the well-kept lawn there, the fresh flowers on the grave of her mother.

"Someone's been here? I wonder who? I mean...who would put flowers on Mother's grave?"

Rusty smiled and turned her so he could look into her face...."Me."

"You?" She gasped looking into his eyes. "But how could you. You've been with me..." Then it dawned on her. "Oh...the cell phone huh?"

He nodded.

"The house looks beautiful Rusty," she whispered as he pulled her close.

"Let's go inside."

"Oh, do you think we should?" she asked, peering about as though the new owner might suddenly appear.

"It'll be fine, come on." He said and pulled her by the hand.

As they walked in, Hannah gasped. Nothing had changed. Not one thing. Her furniture was back in the living room. Her kitchen was stocked. And Pepper peered around the door to greet her with a big lick on her face.

"Rusty...what is this?" She asked totally shocked.

"The new owners...are the old owners. We own it."

He smiled as he pulled her into his arms. He picked her up and held her close to him.

"Welcome home, Mrs. Travers." He whispered as his lips found hers in a kiss that touched time.

Hannah melted into his arms, breathless for his kiss. Then slowly, as though it pained her to turn lose of his mouth, she moved her head to look into his eyes. "What have you done?"

"I bought this place, lock, stock and barrel, for you. It's ours!" He said and carried her into her bedroom.

He kicked the door closed and for long moments there were many oohs and ahhs coming from the bedroom.

"Oh Rusty....my love...."

"You know I could grow used to being called.... Hannah's Man."

Pepper lay down in front of the bedroom door, relaxed and closed his eyes. The Travers had come home!

*The End*

## About the Author

I'm a professional writer of romance and children's books. I'm also a poet and short story writer. I'm working on another historical western right now, one mid-grade book and just finished two historical westerns. You'll find a lot of facts in my historical western romances not the run of the mill romances. Check them out.

I'm also a grandmother and great-grandmother who enjoys spending time with her family.

I hope you enjoy my books. Thank You and God Bless

*Rita Hestand*

## *Rita's Other Books*

Beyond the Dream Catcher
Just One Kiss
Ask No Tomorrows
*A Promised Heart*
Be Free My Heart

Western Serial Killer Series
Better Off Without Her
Good Day for a Hanging
Bad Day for a Killing

The Travers Brothers Series
Chief Cook and Bottle Washer
Courting Abby
Hannah's Man
Along Came Love

The McKay's
Raining in My Heart
Ring of Fire
Twelfth of Never
Stand by Me

The Amory's
Heart of the Wild
Sweeter Than Wine
Mail Order Nanny

Singles
Always Remember
Love Rules

Jodi's Journey
Nick's Baby
Pretend Mom
Runaway Bride
Suspicions of the Heart
Wandering Heart

Brides of the West
Heart of a Family
Delivering the Bride
Heart of a Woman
Wanted Bride
This Side of Forever
Shotgun Bride
A Love as Big as Texas
Heart of a Captive
(coming soon to this series)
Where Ever My Heart Roams
In the Arms of an Angel
Bride from Shenandoah
Falling for the Bride
An Unexpected Welcome
A Desperado's Bride

Made in the USA
Las Vegas, NV
20 January 2021

16239536R00111